how to fall in lust with a devil

DECEIT & DEVOTION

LOLA GLASS

To my husband
For all the awesome sex jokes ;P

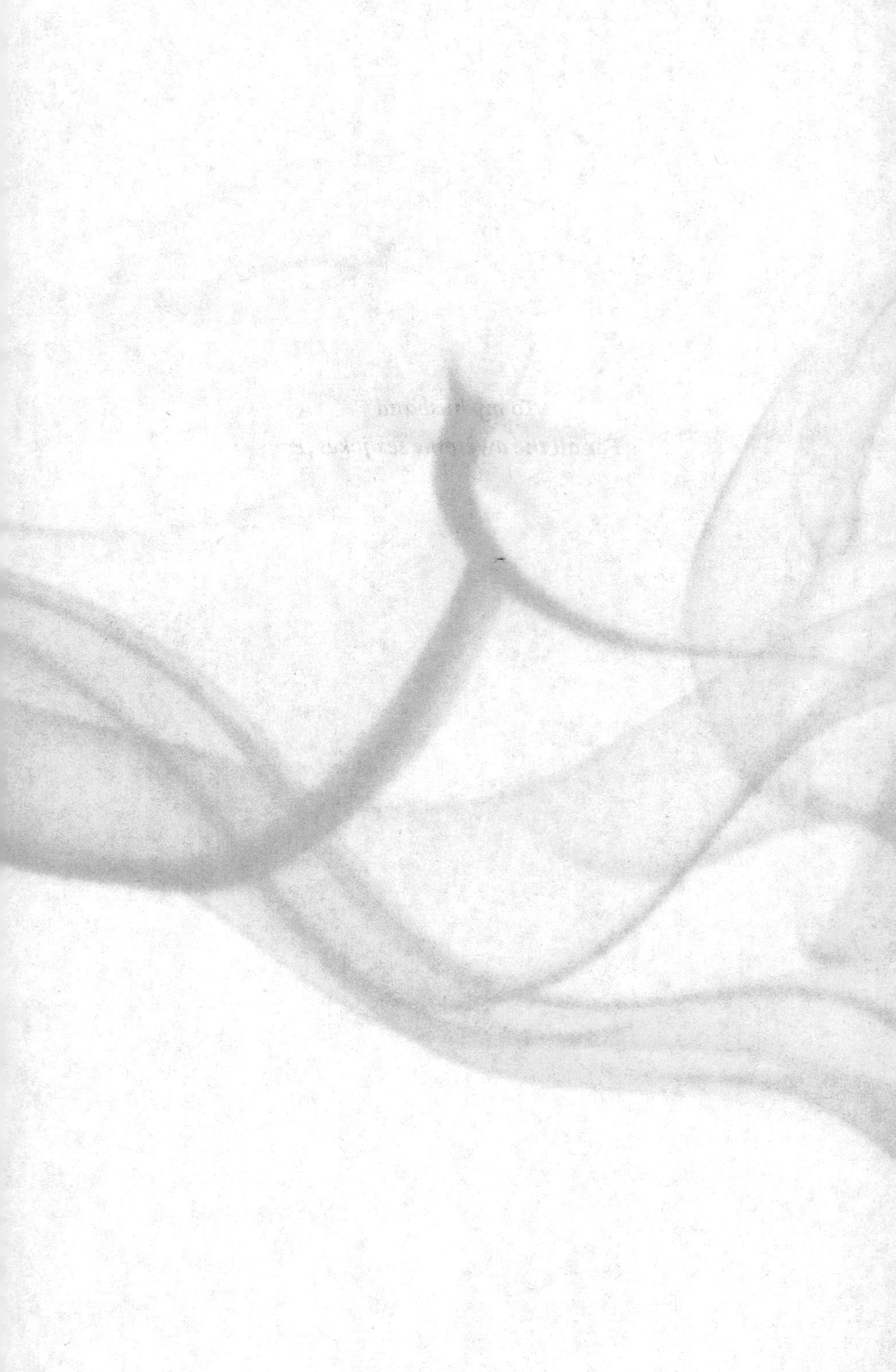

one

BRYNN

THE HEELS of my combat boots scraped the concrete as my older brother literally *dragged* my twenty-five-year-old, curvy-as-hell ass across the cement like I wasn't 5'10" and didn't weigh... as many pounds as I weighed.

But I'm not going to talk about my weight. Weight, schmeight.

It should probably be mentioned that said brother was an ancient dragon shifter. He had raised me alongside my two other brothers, after our parents passed away at my birth, but I was a measly human.

Which meant he was insanely overprotective about *everything*.

Everything that had to do with me, at least.

"This is the most ridiculous thing you have ever done, August," I hissed, fighting like hell to get my wrist out of his hand.

Spoiler: I was not winning the fight.

And my little, red sweaterdress, which was slightly inappropriate for Scale Ridge's freezing Autumn temperatures, didn't appreciate the motion. If I kept fighting, I was going to accidentally flash someone.

"I don't give a damn," August growled back, rapping his fist against the door of the secluded mansion he had literally dragged me up to.

I had a sinking feeling I knew who it belonged to—and it was the one person I wouldn't survive being left with.

Or maybe the one person who wouldn't survive being left with *me*.

"I put up with you moving into my apartment for the last year and watching my every move to prove to you that I was fine. If you do this, it means war," I said, my voice a harsh whisper.

If the house belonged to who I thought the house belonged to, he could probably hear every word I was saying through one of the hundred security cameras probably installed all over the *estate*.

August knocked again, harder.

Then he hit the doorbell and leaned his face down to the camera, growling, "I need a favor, Villin. Do this for me, and I'll owe you."

Everyone wanted a dragon shifter to owe them. The dragons ran the supernatural prison, which meant they could keep someone *out* of prison.

The damn Villins could definitely use that protection. They made it their lives' purpose to hunt down any vampires who went rogue and started killing humans.

I was so fucked.

Or *not* fucked, if you know what I mean.

...Sex.

I'm talking about sex.

Shit, it had been *so long* since I had sex. I missed physical contact, badly. I did still have my best friends, Tatum and Miley, but they were both head-over-heels for their sexy demon mates.

So they were having all the sex.

And I was having none of it.

Oh, how the tides had turned from our days in a shitty apartment, when I was the only one interested in a friendly neighborhood hookup.

Wait... not neighborhood.

That came out wrong.

That's what happens when you try to make jokes after a year of being watched by an overprotective brother.

"Guess he's not home. Let's go." I tried to yank my wrist free from August's grasp, but the bastard didn't budge.

He stabbed his finger into the doorbell again, and ground out, "I will sign a contract swearing not to put you or your brothers in prison. I'm the alpha; the contract will hold. I need your help."

There was a moment of silence.

A long moment.

I could practically hear the gears turning in the head of the one Villin brother I didn't like, despite the walls, doors, and cameras separating us.

"If you do this, I will make it my personal life mission to find you a mate," I finally whispered, the worst possible threat I could give a dragon shifter.

"You will not," he growled back.

"Try me," I was seething. And completely at my brother's mercy. "You will find yourself surrounded by single, human women at every turn. And if I can't pair you up, I'll pair Jas or Eli. They'll curse your name so profoundly, that—"

The door opened, and I cut myself off as a massive presence filled the entryway.

I couldn't suppress the ridiculous goosebumps that appeared on my arms at the sight of him.

Six and a half feet of muscle, gorgeous tan skin, and dark hair that wanted to be wavy but was gelled too sharply to manage it. And all of that was packaged in a black suit and tie that probably cost more than the car his brother had bought me for security's sake.

Sebastian Villin.

My arch nemesis.

Granted, we weren't *really* enemies. His brothers were mated to my best friends, so being enemies wasn't truly an option. He just hated me, and I hated that he lived to squash all potential amounts of fun or joy.

So, we were as close to enemies as two people could get when they were forced to interact semi-frequently and act civil while doing so.

"What do you want, Sky?" Sebastian's voice was smooth, as always.

The man rarely showed any emotion at all. I had definitely never seen him smile.

And I knew without asking that he wasn't talking to me. He never talked to me, if he could avoid it.

Another spoiler: he could pretty much always avoid it.

"I need you to protect my sister. I have to go back to the prison," August said.

Translation: he had decided I needed a large, adult male babysitter while he went back home, because some shit had undoubtedly gone down in his absence.

And the only person he knew who was uptight enough to handle me the way August would himself, was Sebastian.

I was going to *kill* my brother.

"For how long?" Sebastian's question made me want to kill him too. Then again, that didn't take a whole lot, when we were talking about him.

"Indefinitely," August said.

Silence ricocheted between the two men.

"She's human," Sebastian finally said. "Indefinitely isn't an option."

After *that*, I wanted to stab him in the eye. Then strangle him.

I tried once again to pull my wrist out of August's grasp, to no avail.

I didn't need a babysitter—particularly not a big, sexy one who I was very much attracted to but also very much enemies with.

"Thanks, I'm aware of my pending mortality," I snapped. "At this point, I'm used to aging while everyone else around me stays exactly the same."

Both men looked at me.

Then looked back at each other.

"A year," August said. "Give us a year to figure it out. Then, me or one of my brothers will be here at all times to protect her."

Was he kidding?

I hoped he was kidding, even though I was positive he wasn't.

Sebastian was silent for another long moment.

Finally, he jerked his head. "One year. Come in and write up the document."

August dragged me inside the house, slamming the door shut behind me. I was well aware that making a run for it wouldn't do me any good.

"Get me paper, then show her to her room while I work on the document," August said.

Finally, the bastard let go of my arm.

I followed Sebastian down a hallway, rubbing at my wrist while I took in the house. It was pretty, no doubt about it, but everything looked so cold. It reminded me of a medical office, with everything stiff and shiny.

We made it up a staircase before stopping in a doorway at the end of a hall. Sebastian opened the door—and I immediately noticed the way his eyes narrowed at the red skin where August had been holding me.

He grabbed my arm without letting me into the room. "The dragon did this?" His words were still neutral, despite the anger in his eyes.

"Don't worry about it. I'm fine." I pulled my arm away from him.

Unlike my brother, Sebastian let go when I asked.

"If he's ever hurt you…" Sebastian's voice was low and deadly.

"Dragon shifters can't—" I began, before the magic forcing me not to spill dragons' secrets set in. "Dragons like treasure," I bit out, annoyed by the magic. "Family is treasure. They protect it any way they can. Dragging me here is his way of doing that. He'd kill himself before he'd ever hurt me; brothers are just rough. I'm sure you know that."

I put an end to the conversation, stepping into the room. "This is where you want me to sleep?" It was just as cold and lifeless as the rest of the mansion. Dark brown floors. White walls. Large, abstract art placed what a designer would probably call strategically.

To me, it was just boring.

"Yes. I'll pay someone to pick up your stuff today."

I scowled at him. "I'll pick up my own shit. I might not have been able to make my brother leave, but I'm tired of playing prisoner in the name of protection. As you kindly pointed out, I only have one human lifespan, so I'm going to live the hell out of it. Now, get out of *my* room."

Sebastian blinked at me, like he was surprised that I'd stood up for myself, and I shut the door in his face.

When it came to me and my friends, I was known to be the cheerful, nice one.

But that was with people I liked. I didn't like Sebastian. If he was participating in August's protective shit, I wasn't going to force myself to act like I was his friend.

He had never bothered acting like he was *my* friend.

I leaned my back against the door, squeezing my eyes shut.

What the hell was I going to do?

THERE WAS a knock on my door a few minutes later.

It was safe to assume it was either August or Sebastian, and I didn't want to talk to either of them.

"Brynn?" a woman's voice was on the other side of the door.

Was that...

I tugged it open, my eyes lighting up when I found Anastasia Villin on my doorstep. Though she was Sebastian's, Rafael's, and Zander's mom, she was an immortal demon, and therefore would always look young and gorgeous. She had tan skin, and sleek black hair that fell to her ass, thick and smooth. Her eyes were the same gorgeous blue as her sons', and she had a body to kill for.

While I didn't like her oldest son, I *loved* her.

"When did you get here?" I asked, my mood lifting immediately. "How long are you staying?"

Having a big, sexy babysitter wouldn't be so bad with Anastasia there to keep me company. We could chat for ages.

She grinned. "I flew in a few days ago. It's time for me to find Bash a mate."

I snorted at the thought of the big, angry bastard with a woman, then threw my hand over my mouth, eyes widening. "I'm sorry. That was so rude."

She laughed. "Rafael and Zander did the same thing when I said as much. He has a potential mate in the city, though. If I stay long enough, I'm sure he'll accidentally give something away."

I lifted an eyebrow. "He's not exactly an open guy."

"Oh, I know. So far, he hasn't even agreed to leave the house with me. Eventually, I'll get him out. What are you doing here?"

I grimaced at that. "It's a long story."

She gestured to a couch outside my room, in a sitting area of sorts. I sat down with her there, and launched into the story.

She already knew that my best friend, Miles, had been turned into a vampire. She also knew that August had found out about it and flipped his lid, insisting on moving in with me.

But, she didn't know that he'd been debating leaving for the past few months for undisclosed reasons, or that he'd gotten a call about some shit that hit the fan.

Or that he made me get in his car and drove me to Sebastian's mansion. Or that the Villin literally traded me for his family's permanent freedom. The dragon shifters ran the prison—if they refused to take a supernatural, there was no one else to do it, and they walked free.

They never refused to take anyone.

Not that I knew of, at least. But they never told me anything, if they could help it.

"Well, we're both in a predicament," Anastasia said, a wicked gleam in her eyes that I loved. "I'd say it's the perfect opportunity to work together."

"What do you have in mind?" I leaned toward her.

"He won't keep you trapped here; he'll treat you like you're a client he's bodyguarding. He used to do that before the boys started up their side-gig, which I know nothing about." She cut me a look that said she knew everything about it.

"So, he'll follow me around wherever I go?" I checked.

"Yes. We'll make up excuses to explore the city, so we can see how he responds to different locations. There should be areas he tries to avoid. When we've narrowed it down, we'll focus on finding which parts of those locations he's particularly against going to."

She finished, "When we have that figured out, it should be easy enough to find his mate. He won't be able to take his eyes off her after he meets her; she'll be the most gorgeous creature in the world to him."

Well, that was adorable, even if I had a hard time imagining Sebastian being unable to take his eyes off someone.

I didn't even know what to think his dream woman would look like. An athlete, maybe? Small, and toned?

Definitely not like me.

A guy like him would be looking for hard edges and tough chicks. And I knew how to protect myself, but other than one yoga class with my best friends every week, that was the extent of my fitness escapades.

But, anyway, there was no point in dwelling on it. I'd help Anastasia because I liked her, and because it might be kind of fun.

...And because I had a plan of my own that would probably require her help in slipping away from Sebastian for a bit.

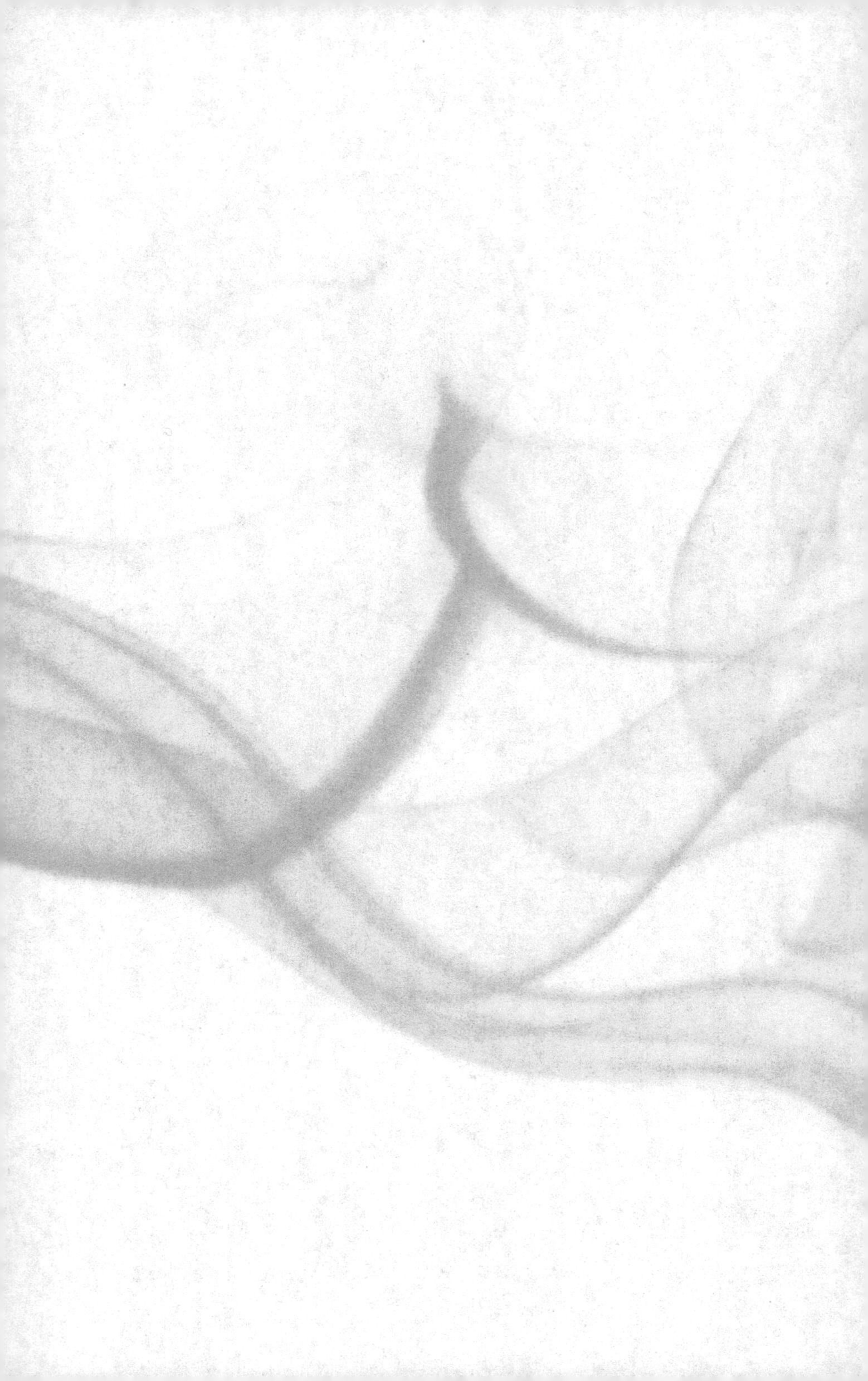

BRYNN

I KICKED off my genius plan by texting Miley that afternoon.

ME

Does Zander monitor my texts?

MILES

...Should he?

ME

NO

I'm just curious

MILES

I'm a little concerned now

ME

Don't be.

August dropped me off at Sebastian's house and assigned him as my new brother.

MILES

WHAT?

ME

Overprotective can recognize itself in the mirror, I guess

MILES

When did this happen? Have you told Tatum?

ME

Earlier today. And no, I've been hatching an evil plan with Anastasia.

MILES

Ah, I see. The mate plan.

ME

Mmhm

MILES

I've tried picturing him with a woman, but I just can't see it. Maybe he'd fit better with a guy?

ME

I don't particularly care who he ends up with as long as he gets TF out of my hair. A mate could help with that.

MILES

Good point.

Zander doesn't monitor anyone's texts. He only reads mine because he's nosy, and I told him it's fine. If he needs to, he can get in easily, but he doesn't otherwise. Bash doesn't know how to hack. Your evil plan should be safe to message about.

ME

Perfect! Thank you!

She sent me a kissing emoji, and I pulled up the conversation I'd been planning to start again as soon as August was gone.

ME

Hey boo, it's been a minute. Want to meet up sometime soon?

RED

What do you need?

I bit my lip.

ME

A big favor.

RED

How much blood is involved?

ME

...All of it?

RED

You're going to get me killed, woman

ME

I'll make it worth your time ;)

RED

Fine. I'll meet you at the club on Thursday. Not a big deal to get everything done in a booth.

I sent him a thumbs-up, followed by the same kiss emoji.

My best friends were going to be pissed as hell, but they'd get over it.

Eventually, at least.

They didn't understand the difficulty of being protected by people bigger and stronger than you for your whole life. They didn't know what it was like not to have basic freedom, and not to be able to make your own decisions.

As much as I loved and understood my brother, I hadn't been able to live my life freely since the day he moved in with me. And I was *never* going to let myself be put in that position again.

So, it was time to make my move.

To make a measured (if slightly insane) decision that would change my whole damn life.

I SPENT the next two days exploring the city with Anastasia. We ate. We shopped. We joked. We laughed. It was honestly a great time.

When I told her I needed to get out for the evening to spend some time with a male friend, she was all-in. She helped me leave a window open (no questions asked, thankfully) and promised to distract Sebastian for as long as she could.

When she texted me that it was clear, I slipped out the window. The fall was kind of high, but I was tall, so it was fine. My knees would ache for a minute, but I'd survive.

I made it to the Uber waiting, tucked myself into the back seat, and grinned as Sebastian's house disappeared behind me.

That would never have been possible with August on my ass.

I officially owed it to Anastasia to find Bash's soulmate. I wasn't sure how easy that would be. I'd likely end up locked in his house until August came back for me, after what I was about to do.

But hey, I'd figure it out.

I massaged my aching knees and replied to comments on our coffee shops' social media pages during the drive into the city. The distance wasn't terrible—about twenty-five minutes—and I needed the time to work, anyway. My best friends and I ran a handful of coffee/candy shops named *Coffee & Toffee*, and I was in charge of ads and social media.

At one point, I'd handled making all of the candy too, but thankfully, that was over.

Tatum and Miles texted me to ask how the evil plan with Anastasia was going, but I left their messages unanswered.

I'd talk to them after it was over.

When I didn't have to lie to them.

I hated keeping secrets, but there was no way around it. If they knew what I was about to do, they would do whatever it took to stop me.

As much as they tried, they couldn't understand what my life had been like. I couldn't explain it to them either, thanks to the magic keeping me from spilling my brothers' secrets.

But I had spent twenty-five years as an outsider. Living a human life while the people I loved most in the world didn't change in the slightest. When my best friends, who were basically my sisters, became demons?

I was done with my humanity.

Transforming into a vampire was simple enough. Miles rocked it, after the initial rough start, and I was sure I could handle it too.

So, I slid my phone in the pocket of my short, tight, glittery blue dress, and slipped out of the car. My usual combat boots made the sparkles more kick-ass, which I loved.

Red had left my name with the bouncers, so I strode past the line. They let me in without batting an eye, and I went straight for the booths.

I didn't need liquid courage in the form of alcohol to make the decision.

I'd known my options for the entire year August had been living with me, and had made my mind up months earlier. There was no question what I wanted.

Red was waiting for me against a wall near the booths. Unlike me, he had a drink in his hand. He was tall, like all supernatural men, with dark skin and gorgeous curls cropped short. He wore a pair of dark jeans, and a gray tee.

"Hey, Gorgeous," he called, his eyes sweeping up and down my figure as I approached.

"Hey yourself." I flashed him a smile.

"You know you're insane, right?" His eyes lingered on my tits before lifting to my throat and remaining there for a minute.

I laughed. "I know."

When I slipped my hand in the crook of his elbow, he didn't hesitate to lead me to the nearest empty booth. My shoulders were back, my body was loose, and my heart...

It was hopeful.

Finally, I was going to be free. Free enough that no one would ever control me again—including the brothers I loved so damn much.

three

BASH

"WHAT DO YOU THINK? Red and gold, or red and pink?" my mother asked, working in the kitchen with my dad while they made dinner together.

The woman hadn't ever asked for my opinions on colors. She didn't *want* help planning her parties. Not from me, at least.

Which was why I was checking on every aspect of my security system, making sure everything was working properly in the app Zander had made for that purpose.

It was no secret that my mother and Brynn were working together to try to find my potential mate. Because it was a pointless endeavor, I wasn't going to try to stop them.

I *was* going to make sure there wasn't another layer to their plan. One that involved Brynn trying to slip away from me.

My finger paused when I reread an alert from a few hours earlier.

My mother had opened a window in her room that morning.

I'd thought it was harmless when the message first came through, but I'd never been informed of it closing.

Shit.

There was a thread in my mind that led me to my potential mate. Every demon had one, when he was near enough to him or her. Mine had been leading me to Brynn since the first moment I stepped into Scale Ridge.

I let my mind follow the thread, expecting to find my female in my home.

Where she was safe.

Instead, it was... moving away from me.

"Where is Brynn going?" My words came out a growl. I usually made an effort not to let the more animalistic side of myself free, but sometimes it couldn't be helped.

Sometimes, meaning, *when Brynn was involved.*

My parents' attention both jerked to me.

My furious gaze met my mom's. "You left your window open for her. Where is she going?"

My chest was tightening.

Fuck, my whole body was tightening.

I didn't know who she was with.

She wasn't protected.

"She's meeting up with a friend. Give her a break, Bash. She's been stuck with her overbearing brother for the past year," my mother finally said, turning back to her pasta.

"Which friend?"

"I didn't ask. Who she spends her free time with is her business. She hasn't been in danger for over a year; leave her be."

If it were Tatum and Miley, she wouldn't have needed to slip out.

"She's meeting a man?" I nearly roared.

I would kill him.

I would rip his heart from his fucking chest if he touched her.

"You're not her brother, Bash. Let the girl have some fun," my dad said, his voice light.

I saw red.

"Of course I'm not her fucking brother, I'm her—" I barely managed to cut myself off before I said *mate*.

The damage was done, though.

I saw the realization hit them both before I stormed out of the house, my phone abandoned on the kitchen counter.

• • •

I HAULED ass down the highway, heading for the city.

I needed to move closer. If I could stomach the people, and the noise, I already would've done so.

Though I made up an assload of ground, it wasn't enough.

In my mind, I felt it as Brynn stopped in the middle of Scale Ridge, at a nightclub owned by the city's vampire clan.

Our relationship with the clan was a reluctant one. They had killed an old family friend, Charlie. The new leader had strict rules against hurting humans, though, so my brothers and I had formed a reluctant peace agreement with him.

Brynn was five minutes ahead of me.

Images slammed into my mind—pictures of her in another man's arms.

I had never felt fury like that before.

Hatred like that before.

I would kill *anyone* who touched her.

My heart pounded hard, the heavy beating like a drum in my ears as I threw my Hummer into park in front of the club. I flew into the building without a glance behind me.

The bouncers recognized me, and stepped aside.

I followed the thread to a booth.

A booth where I found my mate on a man's lap, his teeth buried in her throat. Lust blazed off both of them, the red smoke thick and heady.

My reaction was instinctual.

I had her ripped off the bastard's lap, freeing her from his fucking teeth, in a heartbeat.

My fist slammed into his face a beat later.

And my hands were around his throat in the next.

"Stop!" Brynn's scream pierced the thick, violent haze of my fury.

My hands only tightened.

He clawed at my hands, his desperate eyes growing glassy, then rolling back into his head.

I couldn't fucking wait to watch him die.

Brynn's body was between mine and the vampire's a heartbeat later. She was saying something—telling me to stop—but her lips were red.

Red with the bastard's blood.

His blood had been in her mouth.

On her tongue.

My hands released his throat before I knew what I was doing.

He slumped against the booth's seat, unconscious.

My hand found her hip.

The other gripped her loose, golden hair.

My tongue moved brutally over her lips, licking away the taste of anyone but me.

She gasped, and I filled her mouth. I wasn't kissing her—I was claiming her. Every inch of her mouth.

Her fingers slid into my hair, pulling and tugging and yanking.

It wasn't enough.

My hands moved harshly down the luscious curves of her body. They found the hem of her dress, rolled up to the tops of her thighs, and slid downward.

She gasped again when I gripped her bare ass—then she yanked her mouth away from mine.

The fresh air knocked the common sense I'd been missing into me.

Another minute, and I would've fed from her.

Would've bound myself to her that way.

Would've stripped her bare in the booth, and made her mine with an unconscious vampire only inches away from her bare backside, which my hands were still gloriously full of.

"What the fuck are you doing here?" The demand spewed from my lips, absent of every ounce of the control I'd held so tightly to.

"What the fuck are *you* doing here?" The outrage in her eyes was nearly as thick as the fury in mine. "I don't care what my brother offered you, you don't get to follow me into a nightclub and try to kill the man I wanted to—sleep with!"

She caught herself before she said something else.

I could guess what she was trying to hide.

"His blood was on your lips," I snarled. "His teeth were in your throat. This was a hell of a lot more than sleeping together, Brynlee."

There was only one reason a vampire would give his blood to a human, and it was enough to make me nearly shove past my mate to finish what I'd started with the bastard.

He was going to turn her.

The anger in her eyes told me she was far from innocent in the matter.

"Get out." She pointed to the nightclub's exit. "Now."

"Fine." I grabbed her by the waist and threw her over my shoulder, striding toward the door. Her shriek was drowned out by the loud beat of the music, and her fists pounded against my back.

Though there were dozens of eyes on us, the bouncers just nodded at me as I passed them.

No one dared approach as I dropped my female in the passenger seat of my Hummer, buckled her in, and slammed the door behind her.

She tried to get it open, but I'd already flipped the child lock.

And a moment later, we were peeling away from the club.

Brynn gave up on the door, slamming her head against the back of her seat. "I'm going to find your potential mate," she said, her voice shaking.

I was fairly confident it was shaking with anger. There wasn't a chance her anger could rival mine; I could barely see straight.

"I'm going to get you trapped in a mate bond you don't want, addicted to a woman who doesn't want you either. You think you get to control me—and you're wrong."

My fingers tightened on the steering wheel.

I clenched my jaw to stop myself from telling her that all she had to do was look in the damn mirror to find my woman.

Or that I was hopelessly attached to her already, fighting every instinct I had just to stop myself from taking things further with her.

I didn't want to *control* her.

I wanted to taste every inch of her body.

To drink from her until I was lost entirely.

To fill her.

To make sure she'd never want anyone else but me.

And I couldn't have any of it.

So I clenched my jaw tighter, and didn't let myself say another word.

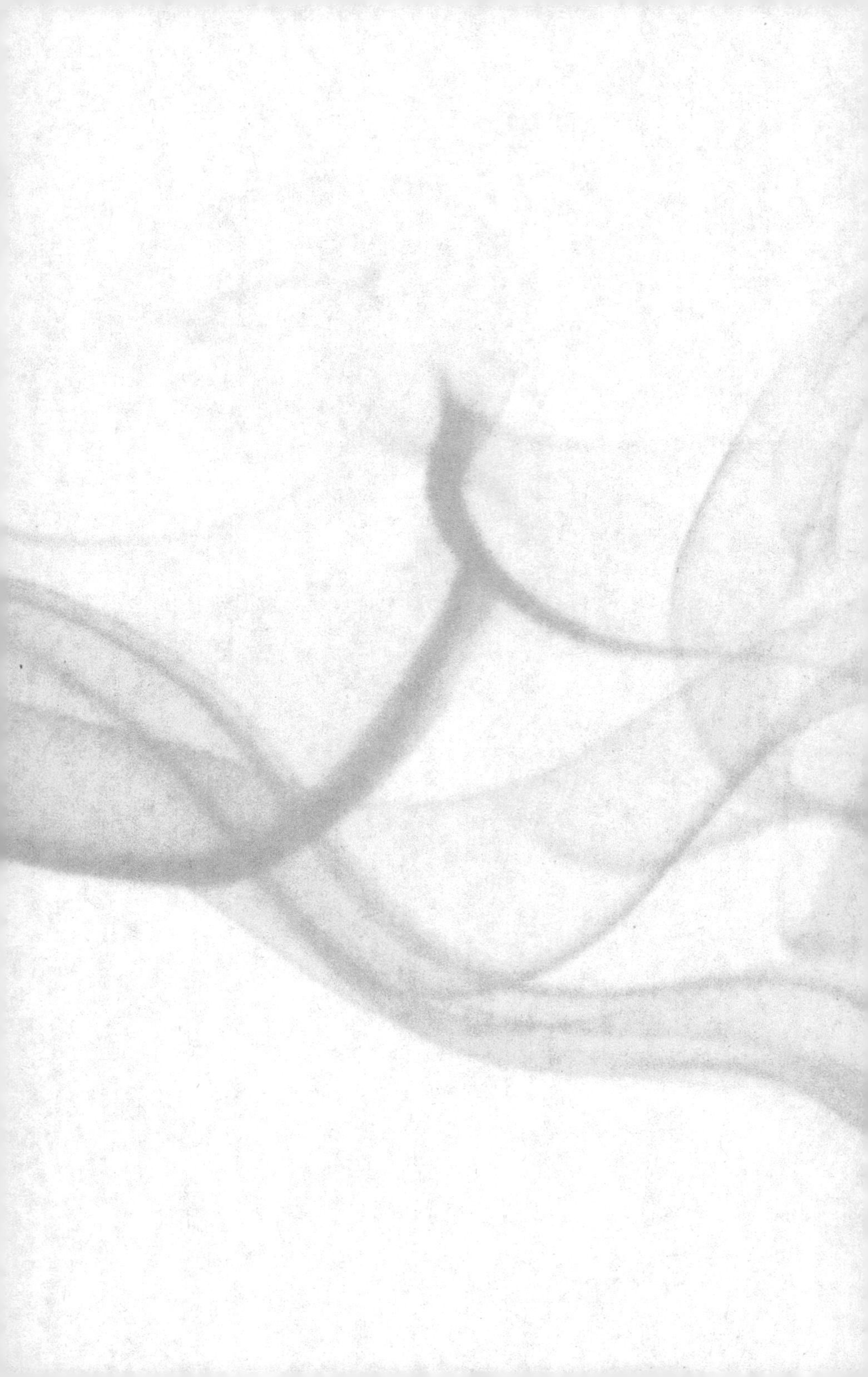

BRYNN

SEBASTIAN OPENED my door to let me out, told me stiffly not to leave again, then disappeared into the house.

When I glumly made my way inside, I found his parents sitting in the gorgeous, gigantic kitchen.

It was just as lifeless as the rest of the house.

Just as cold.

Just as heartless, too.

My eyes stung when I saw the apology on Anastasia's face, and I just murmured a hello before slipping past them.

I couldn't muster up anything else.

I was tired.

I was sad.

My shoulder hurt like hell, the torn skin and aching wound hidden by the hair basically glued to it with blood.

My thong was still drenched with my desire, and my lower belly cramped with need that obviously wouldn't be met by anything except my vibrator.

My one plan to change my life for the better was gone. There wasn't a chance in hell I'd be able to convince Red to turn me after what Sebastian had done to him.

The vampire was alive—I'd seen his chest rising and falling steadily—but there weren't many vampires ballsy enough to go up against the Villins. I sure as hell didn't know any of them.

Red had been my only connection, and now that he knew who I was connected to, he'd never talk to me again. Turning me was even less likely.

There was no doubt in my mind that Miles would refuse to turn me too. Even if she could drink my blood without getting sick, she wouldn't do it.

On top of all that shit, I didn't know why Sebastian had *kissed* me.

And grabbed my ass.

And felt up my body in that hot, possessive way I'd never imagined being touched.

I was getting hot all over again, just thinking about it.

Anastasia's hand caught my arm as she fell into step beside me, matching my pace. "Do you want to talk about what happened?"

My throat swelled.

Yes.

No.

Maybe?

I had no idea what I wanted, other than my freedom.

"I don't know," I finally whispered. "I think I just want to take a hot shower."

Anastasia slipped into my bedroom with me, and closed the door behind us.

I had everything riding on being turned into a vampire, so when I'd gone back to my apartment, I hadn't packed up my stuff. I'd just grabbed a few changes of clothes.

She turned the shower on for me, then waited in the bedroom while I washed up. The wound on my neck was gnarly, and still bleeding a bit when I dried off. I didn't find any bandages in the bathroom, so I just patted it carefully with one of the dark towels and hoped for the best.

After I put on a soft, black *Coffee & Toffee* tee and a pair of shorts, I folded myself into a huge, black decorative chair that was shaped like a corner. It was more comfortable than it looked, though it needed a cute throw pillow or something to bring it to life.

Anastasia was already sitting in the identical one beside it, so I leaned my head back against the cushions and closed my eyes for a minute.

She didn't push or prod for information, which I appreciated.

"You can't tell anyone," I finally whispered. "But I had talked to my only vampire friend, other than Miles, about turning me. He was going to do it tonight. I've been planning to go through with it whenever August left."

It was early November, so I'd known I wanted to be turned for six months, and had been considering it for much longer.

Anastasia didn't say anything in response.

I didn't open my eyes to see the judgment on her face, adding, "I know it sounds insane. I know it *is* insane. But my brothers are immortal, and my best friends are too. I don't have anyone else. I don't want to grow old alone, or die alone."

"That's not insane at all, Brynn." Anastasia's voice was soft, but genuine. "I would do the same if my family was going to live on without me."

Her words eased the tightness in my abdomen, just a little.

"What happened at the club?" she asked.

"I bit Red, then he started draining me. The lust set in because of his bite, as expected. Out of nowhere, Sebastian showed up and ripped me away from him. I've never seen him lose control before—he was like a completely different person. He almost killed Red. I thought he was going to. I shoved myself between him and Red, trying to stop him, and he did the most random thing."

My face flushed, probably insanely pink. "He *kissed* me. I pushed him away after a minute, and when I told him to leave, he threw me over his shoulder and carried me out of the club."

Anastasia was silent again.

I opened my eyes, and found her expression thoughtful.

Maybe even a little wicked.

"You don't look surprised," I said.

"I'm not." She studied me for a moment before saying, "I figured out why he hasn't tried to avoid any particular part of the city."

I blinked.

She was very invested in finding her son's potential mate, but it seemed like a random change of subject.

"Okay..." I trailed off, not entirely done talking about the fact that he had kissed me after ruining my plan.

"He's been too busy avoiding *you*."

"What do you mean?"

She leaned toward me, her long hair falling over her shoulder and resting on her legs. "When you're forced to be in the same room together, what does he do?"

"He stays as far away from me as possible." I was already putting the pieces of what she was saying together, and it scared the hell out of me.

"Does he look at you?"

"No."

"Does he talk to you?"

"Not if he can help it."

"Yet, do you know what happened the moment he realized you were gone? He didn't know about your plan to become a vampire—he flew after you like hell was on his heels, because he realized you were going to meet another man. We couldn't find his potential mate, because *you're* his potential mate."

I squeezed my eyes shut again. "Shit."

"Mmhm." She set her hand on my knee and squeezed lightly. It was still a little sore from my jump out the window.

"This is bad," I said softly.

"Or it's the best thing that could possibly happen."

I opened my eyes, my forehead wrinkling. "How do you figure that?"

"Think about it, Brynn. You want to live as long as the people you love, and to be free of your brothers' control. I want my son to have the stability of a sealed mate bond."

"If we were mated, Bash would be just as controlling as my brothers are. Have you met him?" I gestured toward the door, refusing to acknowledge how easily the nickname he'd never given me permission to use just slipped out. "He chased me to a nightclub, hauled me back here, and told me not to try to leave again. I'm basically a prisoner."

"The bond isn't settled. He's been fighting it for the entire year he's known you. And he takes after Eldrich; it takes a lot more to sate his hunger than it does for most demons. He's hungry, desperate, and at war with his mind and body. Settle him, and all of that will change." Her voice was eager. Way too eager.

I scoffed. "He tries not to *look* at me. Even if I wanted to seal the mate bond—which I don't—it wouldn't work. The man's basically a statue."

"Did he feel like a statue when he kissed you?" The look in her eyes was still so damn wicked.

She leaned in and wrapped her arms around me for a quick, fierce hug. "Eldrich and I booked a flight that leaves early tomorrow morning. My work is obviously done. If you change your mind, don't underestimate your power, Brynn. He's fighting every urge to stare at you, touch you, and take care of you. You're the most stunning creature in the world to him, remember? Make him fight hard enough, and eventually, he'll crack."

Though I was still in shock after our conversation, I hugged her back. "Thanks, I guess."

She whispered, "Don't forget that the man has to eat. He'll be forced to leave your side when he does, or to take you with him. If he doesn't, he'll get hungrier. With hunger comes less control."

"Something tells me he wouldn't want you letting me in on that secret," I murmured back.

She released me with a smirk. "I gave birth to him. He doesn't get to control me any more than he would get to control the woman who decides if, when, and how much he eats. You want freedom, Brynn? Bond yourself to a demon who doesn't take anyone's shit. Including your brothers'."

With that, she slipped out of the room, closing the door behind her.

I sat back against my chair, staring up at the ceiling while her words rolled through my mind on repeat.

You want freedom, Brynn? Bond yourself to a demon who doesn't take anyone's shit. Including your brothers'.

As much as I hated to admit it, I was actually considering her plan.

No one controlled Sebastian Villin.

No one decided where he could go, or what he could do.

No one trapped him in his home or stopped him from finding someone to hook up with if or when he was horny.

No one… except maybe his potential mate.

Me.

And if no one could control him but me, he sure as hell wouldn't let anyone but himself control me. He was obviously too possessive for that.

Being bonded to him *would* be a loss of some aspects of control.

I still wouldn't be able to go to a club, flirt up a storm, and spend a night with someone. I would have to bring him with me when I went anywhere for the first few years, because the demon version of a mate bond would cause psychosis for both of us otherwise.

But we would need to feed on each other's lust after the bond was sealed, so there would be regular sex. Regular *hot* sex, if that kiss was anything to go off of.

And if I was officially a member of the family, my friends and their mates, his brothers, would prevent him from locking me up anywhere for *too* long.

Plus, he traveled a lot for work. That meant I'd get to travel too.

"This is insane," I whispered to myself.

More insane than my plan to get turned into a vampire.

A lot more insane than my plan to sneak away and start a new life for as long as I could hide from my brothers.

But Anastasia was right.

I *did* want freedom.

And I could get it... if I could seduce Sebastian Villin into taking me as his mate.

BRYNN

I WASN'T one for wasting time, so the next morning, I set my new plan into action.

Braless and wearing nothing but my black Coffee & Toffee tee, and a pink lace thong, I padded down into the kitchen. My shoulder still hurt like hell, so I would definitely need to look for medical supplies after the plan was a go.

As expected, Sebastian was there, making breakfast. He was a bastard, but he loved to cook. So hey, he had at least one redeeming quality other than his face.

Well... and probably his dick, if the feel of it I'd gotten last night said anything.

So, three redeeming qualities. Cooking, his face, and his cock.

I had to *act* like I was still pissed at him, though, so he wouldn't figure out my plan.

He glanced over his shoulder at me for a moment before his head jerked back to the food he was cooking.

Victory.

I shuffled into the kitchen, brushing my side against his as I started going through cupboards, checking for what I needed.

"What are you looking for?" His voice was lower than its usual emotionless neutral.

"Ingredients," I snapped back. "One of my new chefs called in sick, and I just found out two of our shops are running low on multiple types of candy."

He was silent for a beat.

I turned, continuing to go through cupboards. My shirt rode up to the middle of my back, so the man was getting a full-on view of my butt and the straps of my thong.

Sure enough, when I peeked over my shoulder, his eyes were on my backside.

I let him stare for a few more minutes before I turned my head entirely, and glowered at him. "Are you staring at my ass?"

His head jerked upward. "What? No. Email me a list. I'll have whatever you need delivered in the next hour." His voice was defensive.

Finally, I'd found his emotions.

If I had to put money on something, I'd bet he didn't know I knew that I was his potential mate. That was kind of a tongue-twister, but it totally worked in my favor.

"If you're going to force me to live here, we need to get a few things straight," I said bluntly, turning my entire body to face him.

My hand landed on my hip, and his gaze dipped to my thong again for a heartbeat before it landed on my face again.

"You don't get to kiss me. You definitely don't get to grab my ass while you kiss me. You don't get to stare at my ass, either. Got it?"

"That won't be a problem." His voice smoothed out, the emotion drying up again instantly.

"I'm picking up the rest of my shit today, after I stop at the grocery store for ingredients myself. I'm choosing a new bedroom too. Since I'm living here, I'll be making myself at home."

"Fine." His word was clipped. "You don't go anywhere without me from here on out."

"Great. I love having a grumpy, handsy companion," I drawled. "Oh, and one more thing. If you ever leave my side, I'm going to go wherever I want and do whatever I want. It's nothing personal, but—well, actually, it *is* personal, since you rudely interrupted me at the club last night. Fuck you for that, by the way."

His jaw clenched.

I flashed him a smile. "Great talk. I'm leaving in twenty minutes. Be in your Hummer, or don't be. I'm taking it either way."

When I strode out of the kitchen, I could feel him staring at me.

"Eyes off my ass, bastard," I called over my shoulder.

He swore under his breath, and I grinned to myself as I headed back up the stairs.

Sebastian was going to *wish* he had gotten to the club too late to stop me from turning.

But Anastasia was right—knowing I was his potential mate made me feel powerful as hell.

I PUT on one of my short, flowy floral dresses, despite the cold outside, and stepped into my combat boots. The zippers went up, then I started opening doors upstairs, looking for a hallway closet that might have medical supplies in it.

Sebastian stepped out of a room at the end of the hallway I was in, and his eyes narrowed when he saw me.

I glared at him, closing the door I'd been looking inside.

"What are you doing?" His voice was back to neutral.

"Trying to choose a room. None of them have any color." I stepped up to the next door, peering inside.

It was almost identical to the last.

"I paid a decorator to buy everything," he said, his voice edging on defensive again.

"So you don't like it either?" I closed the door, moving to the next one and tugging it open.

"That's a closet."

Bingo.

Band-Aids and antibiotic ointment galore.

On second thought, how was I supposed to cover the gaping wound where my shoulder met my neck?

Stepping forward, I started rummaging around, hoping to find a big-ass Band-Aid.

"You said you were looking at the rooms." He stepped up behind me, and I fought the urge to suck in a breath as his chest brushed my back.

I'd been with two supernatural guys before, both of them vampires. Honestly, I wasn't a huge fan of the blood sucking bit. But the size difference? I loved that. There weren't many human men I wasn't eye-to-eye with or taller-than. It had bugged me when I was younger, but I had come to like it. There were benefits to being tall.

But it also felt good to be dwarfed by a man, for some stupid, probably-anti-feminist reason.

"I was. I was just also looking for a Band-Aid."

"Why?" His voice went low again.

I liked it when it was low.

"Some bastard ripped me off a vampire without removing the fangs first," I said flippantly.

Sebastian's chest went stiff behind me.

He moved my hair off my shoulder, pulled my dress to the side, and swore viciously. "Fucking hell. This hasn't healed yet?"

"I'm human," I pointed out, still rummaging around.

"Vampire venom is supposed to heal their victims quickly."

"Vampires don't usually rip their teeth through their food source's neck," I drawled.

Sebastian stepped around me. His movements were violent as he pulled out a tube of antibiotic ointment and a bandage that was indeed big enough to cover my wound. "You should have told me." He yanked the shoulder of my dress further down my arm. My bra strap followed, though he wasn't looking at my tits. "Hold still. I'm taking you to the doctor after I cover this."

"I'm not going to the doctor. I'm fine." I gritted my teeth when he gently covered the area with ointment. He was being careful; it was just sore. "If you really want me to heal, you should take me back to the nightclub and pay someone to turn me into a vampire."

"No one else's teeth are going anywhere near your skin," he snapped.

"No one's except Red's, Crash?" I countered, the ridiculous nickname slipping out.

I'd once joked with Miley that I was going to start calling him by anything I could come up with that rhymed with Bash. He had never given me permission to use his real nickname, so I was going with it.

"No one *else* implies that *someone's* teeth are going near my skin," I pointed out.

"*No one's teeth*," he growled. "Stop moving. I'm trying to get this on right."

I dutifully closed my mouth, though I silently gave myself another point.

I totally won that round.

He had been talking about his teeth being the only ones going near my skin, and we both knew it. Even if I was playing dumb.

"There." He smoothed out the borders of the bandage. "I'll change it when we're back with the ingredients and the rest of your stuff. If it looks any worse, I'm taking you to the doctor, whether you like it or not."

"Fine."

He finally stepped away from me, and I walked to the next door. The one he had stepped out of a few minutes earlier.

When I peered in, I finally found color. It wasn't much; the bedding was navy blue, and there was a rug on the cold tile that had a bit of blue in it too. "Your bedroom?" I checked.

"Yes."

"Your designer didn't choose everything for it." I promptly stepped back and shut the door. Choosing *his* bedroom would probably push him too much, making him take a step back from me. That wasn't part of the plan.

"I changed a few things."

"You're better at her job than she is," I said.

He didn't respond.

I walked to the bedroom almost directly across the hall from his. I already knew I was going to choose it, and had another part of my evil plan brewing.

Opening the door, I looked inside. It had a view of the mountains the other rooms didn't have—which was the perfect excuse.

"The mountain view reminds me of my apartment. I'm picking this one," I decided aloud.

"Great. Let's get moving." He gestured me toward the stairs, and I walked without complaint. "Let me get the doors. I don't want you hurting your shoulder any further."

The request, though grumpy, was sweet.

"I still have one good shoulder," I pointed out, making a show of grabbing the doorknob with my good arm.

He scowled.

When we reached the Hummer, he opened the passenger door before I had the chance, and lifted me into the vehicle too.

That was also sweet of him. And proved his muscles were more than just for show, because I was no twig.

Maybe it wouldn't be so bad to be mated to him after all.

He shut the door behind me, and soon enough, we were driving away.

AFTER A TRIP to the grocery store in which I was also not allowed to push the cart or use my hands to take anything off the shelves (yeah, it got annoying), we made it to my apartment.

My gaze scanned the space as soon as we were inside. I had throw pillows and blankets everywhere.

Maybe I had too much shit to get in one trip. Especially if I was playing along with the story I'd made up about needing to make candy for the shops.

I probably should've just agreed with his plan to pay someone to pack everything up for me.

"This is going to take a while. I'll ask Tatum if she has time to cook today," I announced, ducking into the bathroom to make the call.

When I whispered to Tatum that I needed her to go along with the lie, she agreed without question.

I stepped out a few minutes later. "The bakery is taken care of. Guess we have all day to pack my stuff."

Sebastian was typing something on his phone, and didn't look up at me. "I have work to do at home. We'll just pay someone to handle it."

"Nope." I disagreed out of principle, though his plan sounded way better than mine. "You can sit at the table and work while I pack. I saw a laptop in your Hummer."

He scowled. "Did you bring any boxes?"

I scowled back. "No. Garbage bags will work."

"I'm calling a moving company. Grab anything you don't want them finding."

Though I huffed, I followed his order.

Next time, I'd put up more of a fight.

BACK AT HIS HOUSE, I tucked my vibrator into the nightstand of the bed I'd claimed. Then, I started unpacking the extra bag of clothes I'd brought just in case the moving company took longer than Bash thought it would.

The doorbell rang as I finished up with my bag, so I headed back downstairs.

It was way too soon to be the moving company, so who was at the door?

I opened it up, and blinked at the sight of a gorgeous woman in a *Sweet Dreams* t-shirt. They were the top home-made-candy shop in town, though they didn't have coffee, and were our only real competition in the homemade-candy market. They'd attempted to copy Tatum's seasonal recipes on multiple occasions, so we hated them on principle.

I recognized Cindy, the owner, from her social media pages.

My eyes slid down to the bag in her hand.

The *massive* bag in her hand.

Sweet Dreams charged more than us, and there would've been hundreds of dollars in homemade candy in that bag if it was from one of our shops.

"Oh, uh, are you Sebastian's housekeeper?" The woman's expression remained cheerful. "I have his weekly order here. He usually takes it himself."

Weekly?

He ordered hundreds of dollars in candy from *Sweet Dreams* weekly?

The bastard was going to die.

"Something like that," I said sweetly, plucking the bag from her hand. He would definitely have paid in advance for an order that large, so there was no way she was waiting for cash. "Thanks for delivering this yourself, Cindy. It's not often you find a store's owner making house calls, so we really appreciate it. Sebastian will be cancelling his orders from here on out, but thank you so much again."

With that, I closed the door in her face.

I saw the recognition in her eyes as it shut.

The bitch totally knew me too.

I locked it behind me and spun around.

Of course, Bash was standing at the bottom of the stairs, not far from me. There was something akin to panic in his eyes.

"Want to tell me why you're spending thousands at *Sweet Dreams* every month before or after I tell your sisters-in-law?" I asked him, my voice still sugary-sweet.

Considering Rafael had wanted to sue them after Cindy made her own version of Tatum's last unique seasonal flavor, I was pretty sure his brothers would have something to say about it too.

Though with how thoroughly he had been trying to avoid me, it didn't surprise me at all to find out he would stoop so low just to stay out of my shop.

It didn't surprise me...

But it still hurt.

"Neither sound particularly appealing," Sebastian finally said. "I'll call and cancel."

"You know what? Don't bother." I set the bag of candy on the floor. "Call and ask Cindy out instead, so I have time to track Red down. I've been dying for a good fuck, and she sure seemed eager to feed you."

I pushed past him, and he let me go.

Maybe I wasn't ready to go through with my plan after all.

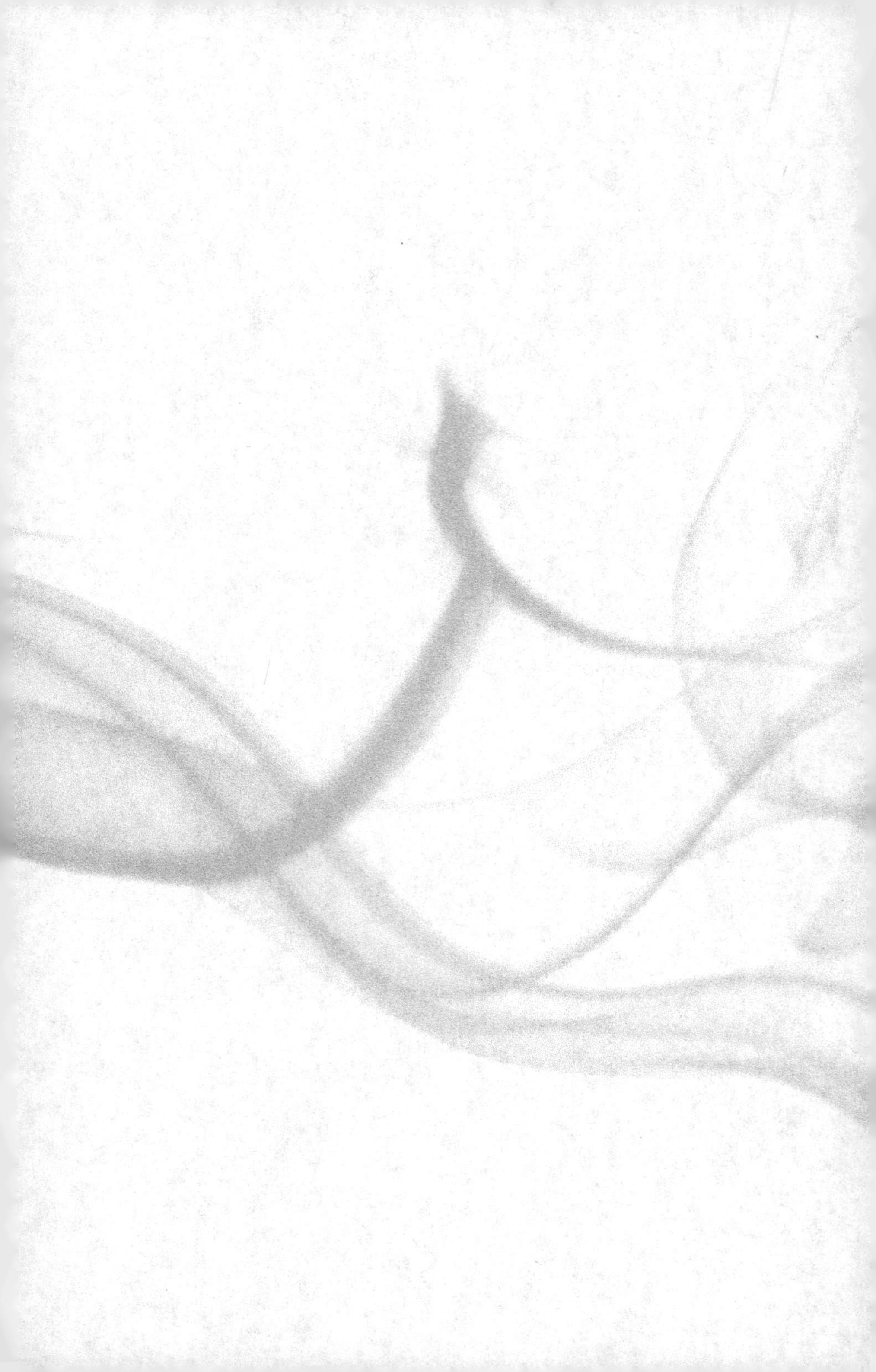

BRYNN

I DECIDED to give myself a few days off from the seduction plan. Mostly, because I was still hurt.

Sebastian texted me a picture of the bag of chocolates in his trash bin shortly after our conversation, but I ignored it.

A picture of his receipt of cancellation with Sweet Dreams came an hour after that. I ignored it too.

Soon after that, a massive order under his name came through my shop's online portal. Instead of confirming it, I hit the cancel button.

He tried again.

I cancelled again, then texted Miles and Tatum to do the same if he tried with any of the other shops.

The girls had my backs.

I felt guilty for not telling them about the potential mate thing, the seduction plan, or the plan to get myself turned into a vampire, but I still didn't know if they'd understand. When I'd had a little more time to grow more confident about everything that had happened, I'd tell them.

Sebastian tried five more times to put an order in with my shop that day, two of them while I was putting my stuff away after the moving company delivered my boxes.

I cancelled all of the orders.

Was it petty and passive aggressive?

Hell yes.

Did I feel bad?

No, I did not.

That bastard had given thousands of dollars to my biggest competitor in his effort to avoid me. He could suffer for a while.

The next morning, I smelled him making breakfast, and stayed in bed.

When he knocked on the door with the food, I told him I wasn't hungry.

I ordered myself an early lunch so he couldn't try the same thing again.

Bash was working on the couch nearest to the kitchen and front door when I went downstairs to pick it up, so I simply met his eyes for a moment, dipped my head in the smallest of nods, and went back upstairs.

He beat me to dinner, so I wasn't hungry again, even though my stomach growled fiercely.

He was still working on the couch when I went downstairs a few hours later. His eyes were narrowed as I grabbed leftovers from the fridge and took them back to my room.

That night, he knocked on my door and insisted on checking my wound. Knowing that wasn't a battle worth fighting, I stepped out of the space I'd claimed, and let him change my bandage in silence.

A FEW MORE DAYS PASSED.

I cancelled more orders.

His eyes narrowed further with every day, and dark circles appeared beneath his eyes.

Though a little guilt began creeping in as time passed, I held firm to my grudge.

The bastard hadn't even apologized.

Repeatedly trying to order a shitload of candy from my store didn't erase what he'd done, or make anything right.

Eventually, I'd restart the seduction plan.

...Assuming I decided to let go of my grudge against him at some point.

· · ·

TATUM CALLED me halfway through day seven of my grudge-holding.

Like usual, she didn't beat around the bush.

"What's going on between you and Bash?"

I blinked, my gaze fixed on my computer screen. I'd been tweaking my ads for too many hours in a row.

She couldn't have known about my seduction plan, and there was no way he would've told anyone how he'd kissed me, so... she had to be talking about something else.

"What do you mean?" I asked.

"Raf said he's acting weird. Angrier than usual. Less rational. You told me not to fulfill any orders for him—I haven't gotten any—so something has to be going on over there."

Oh.

That.

I was silent for a moment. A long moment.

Finally, I said, "I opened the door a few days ago and found Cindy from *Sweet Dreams* on the doorstep."

It was Tatum's turn to go silent for a minute. "He's sleeping with her?" she finally asked.

The idea made me feel violent. "I don't know. She had hundreds of dollars worth of homemade candy in her hands, though. Apparently, he was getting weekly deliveries."

"Bastard," Tatum hissed. "Tell me you killed him so I don't have to."

"I didn't kill him. He sent me a picture of the boxes in the trash bin, and the receipt of cancellation right after. I don't think any more orders are coming."

"Did he apologize?"

"He's Bash. Of course he didn't apologize." I massaged my temples. "I need to get out of here, but he won't let me leave without him. I'm at my wit's end."

"Sounds like he is too, if it's any consolation." Tatum sighed. "I'll ask Raf to talk to him."

"What good will that do?"

"You need a break. He's hangry. A trip to a nightclub wouldn't exactly be a win for you, but it would be better than staying stuck in your room. Besides, you know what happens when a demon gets too hungry, don't you?"

I frowned. "No."

"Sex dreams, Brynn. The sexiest sex dreams in existence. You do not want to experience them unless you have someone to have sex with immediately afterward. Even then, I don't recommend them."

I grimaced, squeezing my eyes shut.

How insulted would I feel if I went to a nightclub with him so he could feed on someone else's lust?

Highly insulted.

But I sure as hell wasn't going to climb in bed with him when he hadn't even bothered apologizing to me.

"I'll have Raf invite him for a night out. Miles and Zander will come too. It'll be fun, B," Tatum said.

I sighed. "Fine."

We ended the call, and I leaned back against my bed's headboard, closing my eyes.

I seriously wished I could've been a vampire at that point. Transforming might have even freed us from each other; Miles hadn't been Zander's mate until after she became a vampire.

A few minutes later, there was a knock on my door.

I wanted to curse.

"What?" I called out instead, not getting out of bed.

"We need to talk." His voice was neutral again. I hated it when he got all neutral.

"I'm working."

"*Now*, Brynlee."

It shouldn't have been hot when he used my full name, but it was.

"Later," I said.

I heard my lock click, and the door swung open. I glared at him as he stepped into the doorway, his posture stiff and his eyes hot.

"No means no, Dash."

"Now means now, Brynlee," he growled back. "You're avoiding me."

"Why *wouldn't* I be avoiding you? Should I list off all the things you've done to piss me off, starting with yanking me off the lap of a guy I was going to have sex with?"

"He was going to turn you," Bash nearly snarled. "And you don't belong to him."

"I belong to myself, and I wanted to be both turned *and* fucked," I shot back.

Bash clenched his jaw.

His fists followed shortly.

His face was paler than usual, and the circles beneath his eyes were getting pretty damn dark. "I need to feed," he said, abruptly changing the subject. "Rafe wants us to meet them at a club in a few hours. We're going."

"Have you ever heard of being polite, Mash?"

"Please," he gritted out.

"Fine."

"We'll leave at eight." He stepped out of the room and slammed the door behind him. I didn't hear his feet on the ground, though. A moment later, the door opened again. His nostrils flared. "I need you to let me buy candy from your shop."

The words sounded difficult for him to get out.

I lifted an eyebrow.

"Please," he snapped.

"Why would I do that? You've made it clear that you prefer my competitors to me."

His eyes blazed with anger. "If I had ordered from any of your shops, you all would've known how much candy I was going through. That wasn't an option. I'm sorry it hurt you."

With that, he stepped out and slammed the door behind himself again.

I grabbed my phone and sent a quick, angry message.

ME

YOU GIVE SHITTY APOLOGIES

BASH

YOU TAKE SHITTY REVENGE

ME

FUCK YOU

BASH

FUCK YOU TOO

BE READY AT 8, AND ACCEPT THE
FUCKING ORDER

PLEASE

I huffed, dropping my phone on the bed and slamming my head against the headboard once more.

I needed to kickstart the seduction plan again, because I sure as hell hadn't been winning whatever was going on between us all week.

Winning at the seduction plan required showering, though.

And shaving.

And definitely washing my hair.

I heaved a sigh, shut my computer, then rolled out of bed. When the order came through, my phone dinged, and I hit the button to accept it.

Bash's next text came through a heartbeat later.

> BASH
> Thank you.

I ignored the message.

There was no point in starting another argument, after all.

AT PROMPTLY EIGHT O'CLOCK, I finished adjusting my bodycon dress. Bash knocked on my door again, less harshly than he had the last time.

I pulled it open, and his gaze dipped to my body.

And lingered.

His eyes heated and narrowed at the same time. "What the fuck are you wearing?"

He looked the same as always. Same hair gelled perfectly without looking greasy or shiny, same insanely expensive suit, and same fancy shoes. Even with the dark circles beneath his eyes, he was still stunningly attractive.

"A dress." I pushed past him, and he let me go.

The man took a sharp breath in when he saw my back.

I knew the dress was risqué. It was black, short, and tight, with horizontal cutouts running up the sides and center. The only bits of fabric without cuts were directly over my tits, vag, and ass.

"I've never seen this dress before." His words were certain, and harsh.

"I save it for special occasions. Since I've been locked in your house for so long, today's a special occasion." My mood was too shitty for the seduction game. Maybe alcohol would fix it.

Or chocolate; I could really go for some chocolate. It had been way too long since I had any candy.

"Is there a jacket that goes with it?" He followed me into the garage.

"No, there's not a jacket to go with it. Should I cover up my ass, since it's not a size two?" I flashed him a glare, and he glared right back.

"You should cover up your ass so every man in the fucking club isn't tempted to grab it."

"Considering the dry spell I'm in, the more tempted they are, the better." I shoved the hair I'd curled loosely over my shoulder, and out of my face.

His jaw was clenched tightly when he grabbed the wheel.

"Is it safe for you to drive right now? You seem pissier than usual." I buckled my seatbelt violently.

"You're never in danger with me." His words were clipped enough not to sell them in the slightest.

It seemed like a low blow to bring up my neck wound that was healing up nicely, so I didn't.

WE DROVE IN SILENCE, his typical classical music playing from the speakers. It was soft and quiet, and made me wonder what he had been like before he started ignoring the mate bond.

Before Rafael went to prison, too.

Before... whatever had hurt him.

Maybe it was ridiculous, but some part of me wanted to understand him. To understand why he had ignored me for so long. Why he'd avoided me, too. Why he was so damn afraid of the mate bond he clearly couldn't fight as well as he wanted to.

But I didn't say any of that aloud. What was the point?

· · ·

"THANK YOU FOR DOING THIS," Sebastian said, after he parked in front of the club.

I wasn't sure what to say, so I didn't respond.

I'd started feeling like a bitch for leaving him hungry, even though he hadn't asked me to feed him or go with him to a nightclub or anything. It had to be difficult knowing you couldn't just walk into the kitchen when your stomach growled.

Maybe I could understand why Anastasia wanted to see her sons mated.

Unfortunately, my understanding meant I was going to have to find a way to restart the seduction plan.

"Wait." His warning was sharp.

I waited in my seat, though I wasn't sure what I was waiting for.

A moment later, he opened my door for me and held out his hand.

Yeah, that melted my heart a little. Or more than a little.

I let him help me from the Hummer, my face warming at the way his eyes roamed my body.

He muttered something that sounded like, "Fuck me."

I almost asked if that was an invitation, but decided against it.

If he was really interested, he would've propositioned me when he got hungry.

Or horny.

Or both.

I'd never been to the club we were walking toward before; honestly, I didn't like nightclubs. The music was too loud, and I would rather dance alone in my underwear than in public, in a tight dress. I didn't like having strangers' hands on me unless I'd traded a few words with them, either.

But it seemed like a necessary evil considering the whole demon thing, so there was no way around it. And hey, I'd still have fun. I could have fun pretty much anywhere, with enough effort.

The bouncers nodded at Sebastian, clearly recognizing him, and let us in without IDs.

I grimaced at the volume in the club as the music pounded through the room. The place was much smaller than the vampire club, but there were still too many people for my taste.

Bash lowered his face toward mine. "Don't let any men touch you, if you want to make it through the night without any fighting."

"Does that include you?"

His lips curved upward the tiniest bit. "If you're smart, it does."

I made a face at him, and he caught my bottom lip, catching me off guard at the same time. His thumb dragged slowly over the sensitive skin.

Someone bumped into us, snapping him out of the moment, and he jerked away quickly.

"Your friends are at the bar. Stay with them until I'm done feeding." His command was loud, but I didn't bother asking why.

The potential mate bond was why.

seven

TATUM AND MILES waved me down from the far end of the bar. I could see the curiosity on their faces, and Bash's brothers' too, from where they were.

Shit.

His back had been to them, so I hoped they hadn't seen anything.

I did still plan on coming clean to them...

I just wasn't ready yet.

"You look hot!" Tatum called, throwing an arm around me for a quick hug.

"Which men are you here to slay?" Miles teased me. She was so much more laid-back since she'd mated with Zander, it was unreal.

I wanted that for myself, too, even though it seemed like an impossibility.

"Whichever ones like tall, curvy blondes!" I exclaimed, taking the stool they'd saved for me.

"All the smart ones, then," the bartender said, grinning at me.

Apparently he'd overheard the conversation.

Whoops.

He was gorgeous, though, with olive skin and long, dark hair tied up in a messy bun. I was probably a little taller than him, but he'd just announced that he didn't care.

"Does that include you?" I teased, leaning over the bar a little.

"Of course it does." He winked. "What can I get you?"

"Just water for now. Thanks." I reached forward to brush my hand over his, but remembered Bash's warning, and pulled back. He caught my hand anyway, lifting it to his lips and brushing a kiss to the back of it before he headed off.

"Well, that was cute," Tatum said playfully.

"What did Bash say to you back there?" Rafael asked, his voice curious.

I rolled my eyes. "He's stepped firmly into August's overprotective role. Guess keeping you guys out of prison is worth another year of my freedom to him."

Both of them grimaced.

Miles and Zander did too, from where they sat on the other side of Tatum and Rafe.

"We can try to distract him so you can sneak off with someone," Miles offered.

"Nah, I don't think it'll work with him. He's insanely protective right now," I called back. "Threatened to kill some people already."

The grimaces deepened.

"It's fine. I can still have fun without having sex!" I grinned at all of them, hoping to lighten the mood I'd accidentally darkened.

Unfortunately, the bartender walked back over with my water and Tatum and Rafael's drinks the moment I said the bit about sex.

"There's a great break room around the corner I can introduce you to, if you want to make it even more fun," he said, grinning even wider than he had the last time.

A large hand landed on my unwounded shoulder. Another landed on my hip. The touch was so hot, it made me shiver.

"Get your manager," Bash commanded the bartender.

His gaze flicked between me and Bash, and he put the pieces together.

Were they the right pieces?

Probably not.

"It's fine," I called out, waving my hand lightly. "Don't get your manager. We're all good."

Sebastian growled behind me, and I cut him off with an elbow to his abdomen before he could say anything else. He grunted at the impact, but let me have my way.

The bartender headed to the other side of the bar quickly, grinning at someone else—and probably propositioning her too.

When I glanced back at my friends, they were grimacing again, alongside their mates.

"Don't fucking touch anyone," Bash gritted out, lowering his lips to my ear. "That wasn't an empty promise, Brynlee."

"I know, geez. Go eat." I shooed him toward the dance floor, and though his expression was tight, he headed back out to it.

"*Something* is going on here," Tatum said, gesturing between me and Bash.

"Something infuriating," I agreed, plucking Tatum's drink from her hand and taking a long swallow.

Maybe the alcohol would help.

"Want to dance?" Miles called out, shimmying her shoulders.

"In five minutes." I held up a hand and took a sip of my water.

Hopefully, Bash could be done eating in five minutes.

On that note, had I eaten dinner?

My stomach growled, assuring me that I most definitely had not.

Rafael glanced down at his phone for a second. "Why is Bash telling me to make sure you get something to eat, Brynn?"

That bastard was so unbelievably obvious.

How had I missed it before?

He had never been so outright protective, or possessive.

Or overbearing.

"I don't know. Gotta pee!" I left my drink on the bar and bee-lined it to the bathroom. Tatum and Miles caught me halfway across the room, linking their arms through mine and walking with me.

The walls separating us from the rest of the club dulled the music a little, making it easier to think, and breathe.

"What's going on, B?" Miles asked me, as I slipped into a stall. There were a few other women around, but everyone was minding their own business.

"I don't want to talk about it."

"Has he hurt you?" she checked.

"Not intentionally."

"We're going to need more details than that," Tatum warned.

I sighed. "Can you just give me a few weeks to figure it out? I'm not ready to talk about any of it yet. I'm not in danger, he's not hurting me, and he's better than August with the protectiveness. So, it's fine. I'm dealing with it."

Both of them were silent as I slipped out of the stall and washed my hands.

"We're worried about you," Tatum finally said.

I threw my arms around both of them, pulling them in for hugs. "I know. I'm sorry. Put a girls' night on the calendar for three weeks from today, and I'll tell you everything."

"Fine," Miles said with a sigh.

"Are you sleeping with him?" Tatum checked.

"What? No. It's weird and complicated, but no. I told you, I'll explain it all in three weeks. I just have to figure some things out first."

"Alright," Tatum agreed, her voice reluctant.

We headed back into the nightclub, arm-in-arm.

"I hate these places," Tatum called out.

Miley grinned, and I laughed. "Me too!"

Sebastian was sitting beside his brothers, all three of their gazes trained on us. Tatum waved, and Rafael waved back before Miles dragged all three of us into the crowd. I wasn't sure how I was going to avoid having some guy's hands on me while we were bumping and grinding and whatnot, but I'd try to keep it as tame as possible.

Zander's arms were around Miles a moment later, his body wrapped around hers as they moved together. He said something into her ear, and she burst out laughing, shimmying against him, and swiveling her hips in a way that was entirely suggestive.

Tatum and Rafael were in the same position, swaying to the music together while they both grinned.

Her feelings about nightclubs had apparently changed, at least for the moment.

A set of hot, huge hands landed on my hips, and I tried to jerk away quickly. "Oh, sorry, I'm really not supposed to—" I cut myself off when my eyes met Bash's.

His gaze dared me to push him away.

My body told me to pull him closer.

I stepped back, and my ass met his erection through his suit.

His grip on me tightened, and I moved my hips.

He moved with me.

Heat rolled through my body, and I swiveled my hips the other way.

He followed me there, too.

The pulse of the music thrummed around us, our bodies rocking together.

Wetness pooled between my thighs as his grip grew tighter, his movements rougher.

The dance alone told me there would be nothing soft or sweet about sex with Bash. He would destroy me—and I would love every damn minute of it.

When the song ended, his lips brushed my ear. "We need to go home. Tell your friends you're tired."

His fingers slowly, reluctantly, unclamped from my waist.

I stepped away from him, my body aching for more.

More dancing.

More touching.

More of *him*.

"I'm going to call it a night," I told Miles and Tatum, throwing my arms around them both. The crowd was still moving around us, but no one dared push the demon men around. They were too big. "It's been fun! Or at least, fun-ish!" I winked at them, and Tatum laughed.

"Let's dance at my house next time," she called out.

"Deal!"

"I'll text you the date for the girls' night so we can get it on the calender!" Miles promised.

Bash didn't grab me again as we slipped out of the crowd, though his body was directly behind mine.

I didn't touch him, either.

We didn't say a word to each other on the way to the Hummer, or when he opened the door and lifted me inside the vehicle.

He took his seat and started the engine. His eyes lingered on the city around us, staying off of me, and I stared out at it too.

A long moment passed before he finally said, "I have to tell you something."

His voice was low, with that tone I loved, but something about the words seemed... colder.

"Go for it." I slipped my shoes off and pulled my legs up onto the seat with me, glad my dress was stretchy despite being outrageously tight.

"You and my mom were looking for my potential mate. She left because she realized she'd already found you—*I'd* already found you. Unintentionally. I've never wanted a mate, so I tried to stay away from you. It's not working anymore."

"I know. She told me, before she left."

He let out a long breath. "Of course she did."

I nodded.

He pinched the bridge of his nose.

"If you don't want a mate, I see two potential options," I said, still staring straight ahead. "You can find a vampire to turn me, and we can go for that. There's a good chance it would erase the bond between us, the same way it created one between Miles and Zander."

He growled at the idea. "No. Your brothers would kill me, and even if they wouldn't, I could never hurt you like that."

"Vampirism isn't painful," I argued.

"Like hell it isn't. Have you ever experienced hunger so intense, you can't think about anything else? It's brutal. It's hard enough being a demon, when all you need is lust—when you need blood, it can seriously alter the way you think. Turning changes some people entirely. We're not taking that risk when there are other options."

"Fine." I still didn't think it was as bad as he was making it out to be, but we could talk about other options. "The alternative is one of us moving away. Far away."

"I tried. Every time I leave, the pull to get back to you is all I can think about. I get obsessive, and the desire is harder to fight when I inevitably lose control to it." The frustration in his voice was evident. "This is why supernaturals move before they meet a potential mate. It screws with your mind."

"I can move somewhere random, where you won't be able to find me. It's not a big deal. I was thinking about moving anyway."

"It won't work. The thread between us is unaffected by distance at this point. I can barely stomach drinking anyone else's lust, and I haven't even tasted yours." His growl was fierce. "The situation is a mess."

"Well, I'm sorry I'm such a burden." I tried to open my door to get out, but the damn child lock was still flipped. When I huffed at him, I found his eyes narrowed at me.

"I'm not frustrated with you, Brynlee. I'm frustrated with the situation."

"I *am* the situation!"

"No. The situation is that I don't want a mate, but I seem to have no choice in the matter any longer."

"With the right woman, it wouldn't matter," I threw out.

"Of course it would. Do you think I enjoy being trapped any more than you do?"

He had me with that one.

If there was anyone who didn't like losing their freedom, it was me.

"Fine. It's not personal, even if it feels personal." I tucked my hair behind my ear. "What options do you see for us?"

"We ignore the bond for a few more years, hoping it will go away, or we embrace it and seal it. Both have pros, and both have cons."

I *loved* hearing there would be cons to sealing a bond with me. Really, *really* loved it.

"Tell me the pros and cons, then."

He pulled out of the parking lot, speaking as he drove. "It will continue to be difficult to ignore the bond for me. I'll be physically pulled toward you even more than I already am.

You'll continue not feeling the effects of it, because you're human. The main pro is that it could potentially fade, freeing us both. The secondary is that we'll maintain more of our freedom, in being able to be apart for typical daily events."

"Alright."

"Sealing the bond comes with more obligations. Even if we decided we're not compatible, there would be no separating. We'd be forced to stay together physically, feeding from each other for the rest of our lives. It would give us stability in being reliant on each other, and there would be no uncertainty left."

"And you would prefer..." I trailed off.

"Not sealing the bond. The pros outweigh the cons for it, where the cons outweigh the pros for sealing it."

Which was why he'd decided to stay away from me for so long.

Great.

"Stability and certainty are pretty big pros," I said, still looking out the window instead of at the man next to me.

"So you'd prefer to seal the bond."

"Yes. Immortality would be a perk for me too, considering none of the people I love are aging, and I am."

"It's not worth the price of constant hunger." His words were sharp.

"Not for you, maybe. I can put up with a lot for the sake of not dying alone."

His jaw clenched. "We'll agree to disagree."

"You'll agree to think I'm wrong, and I'll agree to think you're wrong, you mean." I leaned my head against the window.

It wasn't as if I could force him to give me what I wanted. A mate bond wasn't something I could just drop on his lap. He had to agree, too.

It was just shitty that his refusal meant I was going to have to start searching for a vampire to turn me again. And on the sly, too.

I pulled out my phone and texted Anastasia.

ME

He told me about the bond himself. Says he's not willing to seal it. The plan's dead, I think

ANASTASIA

Is he leaving town?

ME

No. Apparently he can't leave me. Just isn't interested in being with me.

ANASTASIA

Then I'd say the plan is working perfectly.

ME

It seems like a bad idea to try to bond with someone who doesn't want me, though

ANASTASIA

He wants you. He just doesn't want to
want you, right?

ME

I guess…

ANASTASIA

Make him want to want you. Embed
yourself in his life so deeply that he has no
choice but to admit he's not willing to live
without you. That's what Rafael did with
Tatum, isn't it?

ME

Yes?

ANASTASIA

It is. And there are plenty of delicious steps
before sealing the bond. Enjoy them in the
process of embedding yourself.

ME

This probably shouldn't sound like a good
idea, but it kind of does

ANASTASIA

All's fair in love and war, Brynn ;)

I had to bite my lip to stop myself from laughing.

Anastasia was a little wicked… and her sons were, too.

So why not give Bash a taste of his own medicine?

If he was allowed to act like he hated me for the sake of
staying away from me, why shouldn't I be allowed to seduce
him into staying near me?

The seduction plan was definitely back on.

I sent one last message.

ME

> Can demons see/sense lust through a door?

ANASTASIA

If that door is right in front of their face, yes

Good luck :P

My lips curved upward.

Maybe I was a little wicked, too.

BRYNN

I LEFT Sebastian at the front door, fairly confident he would bring me food in the next few minutes. He knew I hadn't had dinner.

There was no point in waiting to kick off the plan again, so I stripped out of my dress and underwear, sprawling out on my bed in the nude.

The door stayed locked, because if I was going to seduce someone as difficult as Bash, I couldn't make it easy for him.

He wanted what he couldn't have.

I'd make myself something he couldn't have, until he snapped and knew he had to have me.

I pulled my vibrator out of the nightstand and lifted it to my clit, closing my eyes and letting out a low moan as the vibrations began.

It had been too long.

I hadn't been able to use it anywhere other than the shower while August was living at me, thanks to my apartment's open floor plan, and I'd discovered I really wasn't a fan of shower orgasms.

Or of forcing myself to stay quiet while I climaxed.

I didn't let myself finish, dragging out the pleasure until I heard Sebastian's footsteps outside my room.

They stopped suddenly on the other side of the door.

I heard a sharp inhale, too.

My lips curved upward, my body rocking as I finally went over the edge. My cries flooded the room, and I heard something hard hit the door.

A fist, maybe.

"Hello?" My voice was breathy when I called out.

He didn't answer.

My lips curved upward, chest rising and falling rapidly.

Ohh yes, I'd make that a nightly occurrence.

A few minutes passed, and I didn't hear him walk away.

Maybe I could be just a little more wicked.

I turned the vibrator back on, and his fist immediately rapped on the door.

"You didn't eat dinner, Brynlee." His voice was gravelly.

"I'm not hungry," I called out, leaving the vibrator on even though I hadn't pressed it to my clit again.

"You eat now, or I'll break down this door and make you."

I shut the vibrator off, but left it in my hand as I crossed the bedroom and pulled the door open. I made sure he could see it as I put a hand on my hip.

His eyes burned down my bare body. They barely touched on the vibrator, lingering on the rest of me.

"Seriously? You wouldn't let me find someone to take me home, and now you can't let me enjoy my time alone?" I drawled.

His throat bobbed. "You need to... eat." He finally peeled his eyes off my tits. They were all but on fire when they met mine. "Food. You need to eat food."

He never stumbled over his words.

I'd successfully caught him off guard.

And, if the tent in his pants was any sign, turned him on.

"I'm busy." I plucked the plate out of his hands, then stepped back into my room, shutting the door in his face.

He still didn't leave.

My lips curved upward further as I sprawled out on my bed, turning the vibrator back on. My cries filled the room soon enough, and he hit the door again. When I lost control, my voice loud and desperate, I heard his muffled curse.

I hoped he touched himself to my sounds.

I hoped he lost control with my name on his lips and my voice in his ears.

Because we were at war... and I wasn't settling for anything less than a sealed mate bond.

THE NEXT DAY, I sent a text to my chef to let her know that I'd take care of the massive online order we'd received, and padded down to the kitchen in my typical thong and t-shirt. I'd have underboob sweat, cooking without a bra, but I'd survive it.

If I was going to embed myself in Sebastian's life after he had announced he was going to keep his distance from me, candy seemed like the best way to go. The outfit was just the icing on the cake.

He was nowhere to be found, so I got to work cooking without an apron on.

That would kind of defeat the purpose of my lack of a bra, after all.

I couldn't figure out how to get my phone to sync with the speaker sitting in the corner of the kitchen, so I just played music straight from it while I worked. My hips swayed and my shoulders rolled, my lips forming the words to the songs while I followed recipes I knew by heart.

When Sebastian finally made an appearance, it was almost lunch time.

I *felt* him before I saw him, his gaze hot on my backside.

"Hey, Hash," I said over my shoulder without glancing backward. "How do I connect my phone to your speaker?"

"There's a passcode. I'll do it." His voice was low again, the way I loved it, and he stepped past me to grab my phone off the counter.

Screw neutral.

He was wearing his usual expensive suit, without a hair out of place.

"Thanks!" I flashed him a smile, and he dipped his head in a nod. Though his gaze was still hot, he'd made an effort not to touch me when he stepped past.

That was fine.

We'd move past it eventually.

A moment later, my music played from the speakers, and a grin stretched across my face.

That was so much better.

I swiveled my hips harder, bobbing my head with the beat as I stirred the contents of the pot on the stove.

"What are you doing?" There was a growl in his voice that made my blood hot.

"Dancing." I winked at him. "And making candy for some weirdo who ordered five hundred bucks worth of chocolate from my shop. He didn't even buy any toffee. Apparently he really likes peppermint truffles, though. I've got enough of them in the fridge to feed an army."

As I expected, the fridge opened a heartbeat later, and Sebastian was biting into a truffle a moment after that.

His low groan made me smile.

The back of his head hit the fridge. "Thank you."

"Mmhm. How does chocolate help your hunger?"

"All sugar takes the edge off. I just like chocolate the most."

"What does it mean to take the edge off?"

He considered it for a moment, taking another bite of his treat while I continued stirring. "You know how when you're truly hungry, and you drink water, it makes your hunger fade for a moment?"

"Yeah." I nodded, body still swaying with the music.

"It's like that."

"And you're always hungry?"

"Always." He started on his second truffle. Or maybe his third.

"All male demons are always hungry though, right?"

"To varying degrees. Personality plays a role in it. Genetics does, too. All of us experience some level of constant hunger, but for some men it's just a feeling that they could eat. For others, it's a feeling of near-starvation that can never be sated."

I whistled. "Damn."

He took another bite of chocolate in response.

"Tatum and Miles have said something about sating their guys before, though. You can be sated, right?"

"In theory."

"You've never felt that before?" I glanced over my shoulder at him, curiosity in my eyes.

"No. I've never found an end to my hunger. My father was the same way, until he mated with my mother."

I looked back at my chocolate. "Even knowing that, you still don't want a mate?"

"There's more to mating than sating hunger, Brynlee."

"Like cooking meals for each other? Or changing each other's bandages?"

He didn't reply to that.

Maybe I'd pushed him a little too much.

"You should probably order from one of my friends' shops next time, to maintain the distance between us," I remarked. "We should take care of our own meals, too. Sharing food is intimate for me. In my family, food equals love."

He didn't reply to that one, either.

After a moment of silence, he finally spoke up. "Did you tell your friends I was sleeping with Cindy from *Sweet Dreams*?"

I blinked. "No."

He handed me his phone. On the screen, there was a text from the night before.

RAFAEL

> If you're fucking Cindy while dancing with Brynn like that, you know I'll have to kill you.

Bash hadn't replied to it.

There was another one he'd left unanswered from earlier that day.

RAFAEL

> Order from Sweet Dreams again, and I'm done working with you.

Yikes.

"Well, are you sleeping with her?" I asked, handing the phone back.

"Of course not." His responding growl was fierce. "I haven't touched a woman since long before I realized I was yours. I sure as hell haven't since then."

Yours.

He said it so easily. Like it was natural and unchangeable.

"You're not mine. You made that pretty clear last night, I'd say." I lifted my pot off the stove and poured the chocolate carefully into my molds. "Tatum called yesterday and asked what was going on between you and me. I had told her not to fill any orders for you, so she figured something was up. When I explained finding Cindy on your doorstep, she asked if you were sleeping with her, and I told her I didn't know. She probably told Rafael about it."

His jaw clenched. "You should've known I wasn't. I've never so much as flirted with the woman."

"We're not mates, so your sex life is none of my business." I smiled sweetly at him, and he narrowed his eyes at me. "Just like how my sex life is none of your business."

"Like hell it isn't."

I changed the subject. "You should probably answer Rafael. He really hates Cindy. He almost sued her a few months ago."

"He *what?*"

"I don't know how you're not aware of this already, but she's been copying Tatum's recipes. She doesn't have them exactly right, of course, but close enough to give them the same name. If we announce seasonal lemon-lavender truffles, she announces them the next day. If we announce peppermint cookie truffles, she announces them."

Bash's didn't reply.

"Tatum tries not to care about it, but it makes Rafe *furious*. She convinced him not to attempt a lawsuit the last time, just barely. I'm sure finding out you've been single-handedly keeping them in business didn't make him happy. If it happens again, I think Cindy's going to have a huge, charming Villin threatening her life."

When he didn't reply again, I glanced over my shoulder and found his fingers flying over his phone's keyboard.

Hmm.

I wanted to ask what he was doing, but figured I'd probably pushed him enough for the morning.

My phone started ringing a minute later, so I finished pouring the last of my chocolate, then grabbed the device.

"Hey, Tatum."

"What did you do?" Her whisper was panicked.

"I'm going to need you to clarify that question."

"You told Bash about *Sweet Dreams*?"

"Yes. I don't know how he didn't know already. His brothers are mated to you and Miles."

"He's been avoiding us. Even if he hadn't been, he wouldn't know. You can't tell Bash this kind of shit—he'll actually do something about it," she hissed.

"Like what?"

"Like *buy the property Cindy's shop is on and evict her*."

"Shit." I glanced at Sebastian.

He was still typing furiously.

"I'll handle it," I said, hanging up and dropping the phone.

Guess I was going to have to push him a little more after all.

I dipped my finger in the chocolate stuck to the bowl, and stepped into Sebastian's personal bubble.

His gaze jerked upward when my body nearly met his.

"Can you taste this, to make sure it's good?" I lifted my finger to his lips without waiting for his answer.

He didn't move at first.

I started to drag my finger over his bottom lip, sort of like the way he'd touched mine in the club, but he didn't give me the chance to finish. He caught my wrist and maintained eye contact as he wrapped his lips around my finger. His tongue stroked the skin slowly, and I sucked in a breath.

His eyes heated as the lust around me probably swelled. I was sure as hell imagining that tongue on other, more sensitive parts of my body. Hopefully he was too.

He was in no hurry to release me, licking and sucking until my knees knocked together.

Maybe he could be gentle after all.

Finally, he released me. "It's delicious." The growl in his voice told me he wasn't talking about the chocolate.

My toes curled. "Since you're so interested in my sex life, maybe you should get intimately acquainted with it."

"That is very difficult to do without feeding." The growl in his voice deepened.

"And if you feed, you'll get addicted."

"Without question."

My lust would satisfy him in a way no one else's ever could.

That thought made my toes curl a little more.

"Guess I'll have to find someone else to take care of my needs, then." I started to step back, but his hand caught my side.

Right below my breasts.

His thumb dragged lightly—so lightly—over the underside of my breast. "The next man who touches you forfeits his life, Brynlee."

"Including you?"

"No. You belong to me."

"I belong to *myself*."

His thumb brushed the underside of my breast again, a little harder, as if that was punishment. "Agree to disagree again."

Argh.

He was infuriating.

And I still needed to steal his phone.

Which meant continuing the distraction.

"What if he buys me flowers first, Dash? You know flowers mean a guy is serious."

"He can buy you as many flowers as you want; he's not getting through my front door, or touching your skin."

I slipped his phone out of his hand. "I'll make a note of that. Only have sex on the porch, and only let him touch me through my clothes."

He growled at me, his hands landing on my hips and gripping hard.

I looked down at his phone, finding an almost-finished email on the screen.

It had the address of a property—which I had to believe was Sweet Dreams—and an instruction to acquire it by any means necessary.

I deleted the draft, and started to slip the phone into my bra before I realized I wasn't wearing one.

Crap.

Sebastian's eyebrows were raised when I looked back up at him, his phone halfway inside my shirt. "What are you doing now?"

"Preventing *you* from destroying a small business." I poked him in the chest, pulling his phone away from my boobs and tucking it behind my back. "I didn't tell you about Cindy so you could fix the problem. Not everything needs to be fixed. I told you so you would understand why you needed to talk to your brother."

"*This* issue clearly needs fixing." He reached behind my back, and I stepped away quickly.

He stepped after me.

I took another step, turning myself so my back faced out of the kitchen.

He followed.

And kept following me—until my butt met the ledge of the kitchen table.

An "oof" escaped me at the contact.

His sharp-edged, modern furniture was a pain in my ass. Literally.

"I'm dealing with it," he said, leaning against me as he reached around my back.

I made one ridiculous, insane, last-ditch attempt—and stuck the phone beneath the strap of my thong.

His fingers brushed the lace, then stilled.

"You've been avoiding your family because of me," I said. "You would've already known about this issue and dealt with it if you hadn't been hiding."

"I wasn't *hiding*." His voice was low again.

"Don't lie to me or yourself, Rash. You're afraid of our connection."

"Of course I'm afraid of binding myself to you for the rest of our lives. I have no idea how to be anyone's partner, let alone mate, or husband."

"You know how to be a friend. We could start from there. Friendship wouldn't screw anyone."

He scowled. "I'm not ready to agree to anything right now. Even friendship."

I ignored the sting of hurt.

All was fair in love and war. I just had to remember that.

"Then I'm sorry I shared anything about my friends and my business with you," I said bluntly. "And if you do anything to hurt Cindy's business, including buying the property she rents, I will throw out everything I've made. Your chocolate supply will be cut off again, and you'll have to resort to the grocery store stuff."

His eyes narrowed.

Mine narrowed right back.

"I'll leave her business alone," he finally bit out.

"Then I'll finish the candy you ordered, and get out of your hair. We'll go with my plan as it applies to meals. We both decide our own eating habits, and feed ourselves."

His jaw clenched. "Fine."

"Great."

A moment passed, and he finally took a step away. His hand went out. "I need my phone back."

The neutrality made me want to scowl.

I pulled his phone away from my ass and handed it over. "Might want to wash that."

He muttered something under his breath as he walked away. I couldn't have heard right, because it sounded like, *"With my tongue."*

Both of us went back to work.

That... wasn't how I'd expected the morning to go.

I'd stick with the nightly vibrator thing until he decided to budge on the friendship bit.

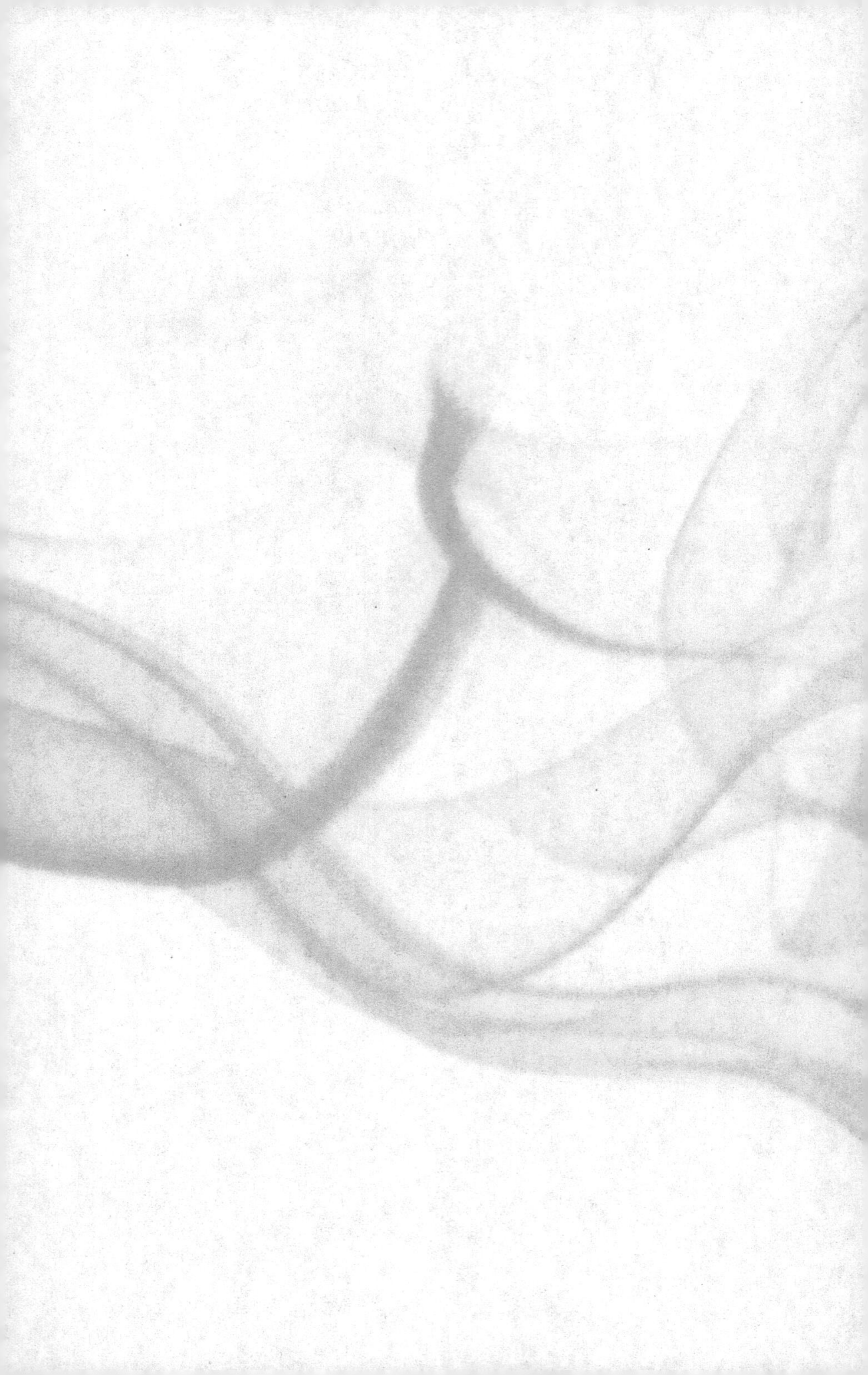

nine

BASH

BRYNN AVOIDED me for the next week. It took every shred of effort I had not to bring her food when she didn't show up for meals. I couldn't stop myself from working on the couch, so I could make sure she ate enough.

She didn't.

Part of me hoped she would offer to make more candy when mine ran out a few days later, but she didn't do that either.

It was my fault.

I shouldn't have told her I didn't want to be friends. It was a lie—one that had probably hurt her.

I felt like shit for it.

My hunger grew worse with every day that passed. Particularly at night, when she used her vibrator, and filled the house with her cries. I couldn't stop myself from jerking off to the sound of her pleasure. It was either that, or breaking her door down so I could make her climax myself.

I WOKE up the morning of the eighth day so hungry, I could barely force myself out of bed.

We couldn't keep going the way we were.

Or at least, *I* couldn't.

I had to apologize and find a way to come to an agreement with her. Friendship would be fine. I'd figure out a way to make it work without losing my mind to it like I had the last time I let myself care about a woman.

Putting in an order for an apology gift, I forced myself into the shower, then into my suit. The fabric felt tighter and more irritating than usual, but my hunger was to blame for that.

I went downstairs to grab the gift before anyone knocked on the door, then headed up to her room and knocked.

When she didn't answer, I knocked again.

Louder.

My mind followed the thread connecting us, proving she was still at home with me.

Her feet finally hit the floor, her footsteps uneven. When she pulled it open, her hair was a tangled mess, her eyelids heavy with sleep. Her Coffee & Toffee tee had rolled up above her belly button, and the tiny thong she had on barely hid the folds I wanted to bury my face in.

Fuck me, she was the sexiest thing I'd ever seen.

Her forehead knitted together when she saw me at her door, holding a wrapped present with a bow on the top.

"It's for you." I held it out. "A peace offering."

She eyed it suspiciously, then looked at me with that same expression. "Why? We're not friends."

"I'd like us to be." I slipped my free hand into my pocket, so I wouldn't be tempted to pull her into my arms.

"You need something from me, don't you, Cash?" She leaned against the door. That damn thong was still tempting me to rip the fabric from her body and get intimately acquainted with my mate.

"I need to feed," I admitted. "And I need chocolate."

"I told you to order from Tatum or Miles."

"It tastes better when you make it." The lie slipped from my lips too easily. It tasted the same—but I couldn't manage to force myself to buy from one of her friends after I'd hurt her so badly by ordering from *Sweet Dreams*.

She scowled. "Liar."

Thankfully, she took the present and started opening it anyway.

The box inside was sleek and black.

I remained where I was, my abdomen tight as she opened it.

Her eyes widened as she stared down at it. Her cheeks went pink, too.

Shit.

She was pissed.

I had to explain.

"You said you needed someone to take care of your needs. I can handle it." I tilted my head toward the thick vibrator in the box. Hers was only made for her clit; mine would fill her, too.

Not as well as I could, but the toy was her only other option, considering what I'd do to anyone who touched her.

She bit her lip.

She was biting back a smile.

Her shoulders shook a little, until finally, she burst out laughing. "Fine, we can be friends." She wiped a few tears away. Happy tears.

My chest burned.

Relief?

Attraction?

Happiness?

I had no idea which emotion fueled the burning. All three?

Clearly, I was in over my head.

If her laughter could make me feel that out of my element, I needed to take a step back. How could I, though? I couldn't even convince myself to leave her damn side.

Her cheeks were still pink, her lips still curved upward in humor. "I'll go to a club with you tonight, but I'd prefer to leave as soon as you're done eating. I don't like clubs. The loud music makes it too hard to think."

"On that, we agree."

At least there was *something*.

"If I want alcohol, you're buying it," she added.

"Of course."

I took a step back, but stopped myself when she added one more thing.

"And if we're going to be friends, you're not allowed to be an asshole anymore. No glaring at me. No scowling, either. You treat me the way you treat your friends."

"I don't have any friends." The words sounded a bit harsh, but they were true.

"The way you treat Tatum and Miles, then."

I couldn't treat her like I would my brothers' mates any more than I could stop myself from staring at her ass. She was *mine,* even if I couldn't act on it.

I nodded anyway.

Her smile was so damn bright. "Perfect."

She started to close the door, then reconsidered, and stopped it halfway. "Thanksgiving is coming up, and my brothers can't get away for it. Your mom invited me to join you guys, but I didn't want to overstep by agreeing, so I told her I'd think about it. What do you want me to do?"

My jaw clenched at the thought of Brynn spending the holiday alone. "I'm not going without you. I promised your brother I'd keep you safe." The second part was an afterthought, to catch the words that slipped out.

It all came out harsher than I intended.

"Great. I'll buy a plane ticket." She started to close the door again, but I stopped it.

"I book the whole row whenever I fly. You'll take the seat beside mine. I'll email you the information."

She blinked.

I let go of the door, and she let it close.

My body relaxed more than it had in a week as I made my way back down to the couch that had become my second office.

WHEN LUNCHTIME CAME and went with no sign of Brynn, I stopped debating internally and sent her the text that had been distracting me for hours.

ME

Now that we're friends, can I bring you
meals when you skip them?

BRYNN

I don't think so. Noticing whether or not I
eat seems a bit more than friendly.

I glared down at the screen.

BRYNN

Being friends would potentially mean we
could arrange a trade, though. I could keep
you stocked up on candy, if you could
bring me one meal a day. I'm terrible at
remembering to have lunch, and end up
eating way too much at dinner to make up
for it.

ME

Two meals a day in exchange for
chocolate. Lunch and dinner.

BRYNN

That doesn't sound fair. Two meals a day is
a lot.

ME

I go through a lot of chocolate

BRYNN

Not THAT much.

You'll have to think of something else I can
add to the trade if you want to feed me two
meals a day and keep it fair.

My fingers moved before I could stop them.

ME

Leave your door open when you get
yourself off at night.

Shit.

I shouldn't have sent that.

I almost hit the unsend button, but knew she'd already seen the message. If I unsent it, she would be offended. Or at the very least, she would know how damn uncertain I was about everything that had to do with her, and us.

> **BRYNN**
> Reasonable trade. Deal.

I blinked.

If I knew she'd agree to all of that so easily, I would've brought her a damn peace offering a week earlier.

> **ME**
> No telling me you'll eat later, or that you're not hungry.

> **BRYNN**
> I won't. What time do you want to leave for the club?

> **ME**
> Whenever you're ready tonight.

She sent me an eye-rolling emoji.

> **BRYNN**
> Give me a time

> **ME**
> 8

She sent a thumbs-up, and the conversation was over.

Despite the hunger raging in my abdomen, I couldn't bring myself to give a damn about eating.

Not when my cock was already hard at the thought of watching my female fill herself with my vibrator afterward.

It was going to be a long day.

BRYNN

SEBASTIAN LEFT me at the bar with his credit card and a warning not to let anyone touch me, then disappeared into the crowd on the dance floor. It was the same club we'd gone to the last time, but none of our friends were there.

I sipped a fruity drink while he fed from the crowd, and thankfully, no one flirted with me.

In any other situation, I'd be a little bummed about the lack of flirting. But considering Bash's text earlier, I was nothing but a bundle of excitement.

And maybe some nerves, too.

Leave your door open when you get yourself off at night, the message had said.

I hadn't even known if he was listening to me. I'd just kept going with it in the hopes that he was. Considering he'd given me the mother of all vibrators—or father, I guess—it seemed safe to say he'd been listening.

My body flushed at the thought that he might've been jerking off, too.

I'd ask him about it, whenever I convinced him to take us from friends to girlfriend/boyfriend. It would probably be a while, all things considered, but I'd make it.

Hopefully, he *wouldn't* make it, and I'd get to see him touch himself.

Although, I was pretty sure I'd never be able to hook up with anyone else again after I saw Bash naked. He was so ridiculously gorgeous.

When we got to the girlfriend/boyfriend point, I'd buy him a pair of sweats. If he had any sense of comfort at all, he'd never wear a suit again after that.

After a few minutes, he came back over to me and tucked an arm around my waist, letting me know he was ready to go. He had the bartender flagged and the bill paid faster than I knew was possible.

The touch wasn't any more friend-like than him watching me use my vibrator, but I wasn't going to point that out to the guy.

"You can't have eaten enough." I looked back at the crowd. I still didn't see lust, obviously, but there were plenty of people.

"I'm fine. Let's go."

"Lash," I protested, "We came all the way here. Go out and eat more. You've been starving all week."

"I'm not hungry for *their* lust, Brynlee." His eyes were hot.

His touch was, too.

"If you want to drink from me, you should just ask," I said.

"I wish I could." He eased me off the barstool, then led me toward the door. When I leaned against him, he tucked me closer to his side.

As much as I got irritated with him, I was starting to understand Sebastian Villin.

He wasn't staying away from me because he didn't want me. He wasn't even staying away from me because he didn't *want* to want me.

He was staying away from me because he was afraid of losing his freedom. Of being rejected by me, not in the current moment, but at a future time.

Of being *hurt*.

And who wasn't afraid of being hurt?

I couldn't hold his fear against him any more than I could fix it myself.

But he'd proven when he came to my door with a present that he was willing to fight when he absolutely had to. He had to eat, so he'd agreed to be my friend.

What would it take before he decided he absolutely had to be my boyfriend? Or my fiancé? Or my husband? Or my mate?

I wasn't sure.

I also wasn't sure I wanted to know.

There was a real possibility that he would never feel that certain about me, and that was scary, too. I wasn't the kind of girl who would stick with a guy who refused to commit to me. I'd give him time to make up his mind, and if he didn't, I would leave.

It would hurt like hell, but I really *was* still human. And that meant I didn't have a decade or two to waste with someone who would never decide he wanted to spend his immortal life with me.

But, I also wasn't in a hurry.

I was stuck with him for a whole year, whether I liked it or not. Afterward, Jasper and Elijah, my other two brothers, would take turns with August in trying to keep me prisoner. I hadn't been able to get away from August, but I was confident I could sneak out from under Eli's or Jasper's nose if I was smart about it.

And ultimately, Anastasia's plan did have merit. I'd give it my best shot before I decided to walk away if Bash still wasn't up for spending our lives together.

It would be difficult to get away from him, too, considering he said he could track me, but I'd cross that road when I got there.

The drive back to his house was relaxing, with his usual classical music playing quietly. I rolled the window down, and let the wind have its way with my hair.

My eyes closed, and I breathed in and out, enjoying the rush of it.

Scale Ridge was beautiful.

One of the hardest things about being born human, while surrounded by dragon shifters, was that I'd never know what it felt like to fly. The dragons lived for it. They did whatever they had to in order to maintain their freedom— even staying single when their bodies and magic urged them to take mates—because of how much they loved the sky.

I wanted that for myself.

That freedom.

That bliss.

Bash's hand brushed my thigh, and I didn't let myself react to the contact. He felt good, but I didn't want to spook him.

As silly as it should've been to think of a massive, muscular man as *scared*, it was the truth. And it wasn't silly. Not to me.

Something had obviously hurt him in the past. I didn't know what, and couldn't ask, but I knew that was true.

Eventually, he'd tell me.

Or, I'd go through with my plan to leave.

I wasn't going to play the seduction game for more than the year ahead of us, after all.

I would encourage him—but I wouldn't push the boundaries he had set. If he wanted things to change between us, he was going to have to make that choice.

WHEN WE GOT BACK to his house, he slipped into the kitchen while I headed upstairs. He didn't have any chocolate left, so I wasn't sure what he was looking for. Coffee, maybe? With a shit ton of sugar in it?

I swapped my tight dress for a *Coffee & Toffee* tee and a thong.

If he wanted me to strip, or to use the huge-ass vibrator he'd given me, he was going to have to ask me to.

Or *order* me to.

Ohh, I liked the idea of that last one.

I was pretty sure it would take a while before he decided he was willing to come inside my room at all, though. The future I saw was full of Bash hovering in the doorway, watching me orgasm with hot eyes and a clenched jaw.

And a tent in his pants, of course.

I relaxed on my bed for a minute before slipping my hand between my thighs. My thong stayed on; I wasn't making anything easy for him.

Or at least, I wasn't making *everything* easy for him.

My breathing picked up, sounds of pleasure beginning to escape me, and Sebastian appeared in the doorway.

He was still wearing that damn suit—and his hair was still perfect.

I wanted to see him mussed.

I wanted to watch him come undone.

I grabbed my vibrator and pressed it to my clit, crying out at the sensation.

My hips arched.

My body rocked.

My chest heaved.

When I shattered, my cries flooded the room, but my eyes were locked with Bash's.

He wanted me *so much*.

But it was his choice whether or not he acted on it.

And he didn't act on it.

He did rake his hand through his hair twice, though, before he stiffly walked to his room. Unlike me, he shut the door behind him.

But I still heard him snarl as he brought himself to release, and couldn't help the satisfied smile that slipped onto my face.

There was no hurry.

Anastasia was right; eventually, his control would break.

TWO WEEKS of friendship went by quickly, with more clothed-orgasms, and not a peep, request, or command from Bash to take my clothes off or use the vibrator. He fed me as promised, I supplied chocolate, and we went to a nightclub so he could feed for a few minutes twice a week.

Anastasia texted me when we were on our way to the airport for the holiday celebration.

ANASTASIA

I'm excited to get the whole family together! How are things going with the plan?

I couldn't stop my small smile.

ME

Not well enough to consider me part of the family yet

ANASTASIA

But there's been progress?

ME

A little

ANASTASIA

Then it's working. I have an idea to make it work faster, too, while you're here.

ME

Should I ask what it is?

ANASTASIA

It'll be better if you're surprised.

I bit back a grin.

Let the wickedness commence.

IT WAS a one-hour drive from the airport to Eldrich and Anastasia's house in California. Rain poured down on us through the whole drive, but my gaze was still fixed on the gorgeous, snow-less scenery around us.

The house was stunning, of course, though it wasn't quite my style. Everything was ornate and intricate.

I liked it a hell of a lot more than I liked the modernness of Sebastian's house, at least. If I never saw another corner-shaped chair, it would still be too soon.

Miles, Tatum, and their mates arrived with us, so there was a flurry of hugs and exclamations before everyone headed to their rooms.

"I'll put Brynn's suitcase in the guest room," Bash said, already striding toward the stairs with his suitcase in one hand and mine in the other.

"Perfect. I should let you know, you'll be sharing your room with Anthony," Anastasia said smoothly. "He'll be getting in later tonight."

Bash blinked.

Zander snorted.

Rafael grinned broadly.

"What?" Bash's voice was neutral, but there was fire in his eyes.

"Who's Anthony?" Miles asked.

"One of our cousins. You met him at the mating celebration." Zander tucked an escaped curl back into her bun, still grinning. "He's a riot."

"Is he the one who stared at Brynn's tits for hours?" Tatum asked, her eyebrows raised.

Rafael choked on a laugh.

Zander coughed, loudly.

Bash's eyes narrowed at his mother.

I barely managed to bite back a grin.

Oh, her plan was *terrible*. I loved it.

"I wasn't watching him at the celebration, but he's always polite, and friendly. He had nothing else to do over the holidays, so I invited him."

"You could've booked him a hotel room," Bash growled.

"It's Thanksgiving, honey. Everything has been booked out for months." She flashed him an apologetic smile. "The couch is open, if you prefer."

His jaw clenched, and he headed up the stairs. His footsteps were a bit violent.

Zander coughed again. When I glanced over at him, I found his eyes watering, he was fighting back laughter so hard.

"Do you remember Anthony?" Tatum asked me, as we went upstairs with the guys.

"Yup. He definitely stared at my boobs a lot. He asked me if I wanted to hook up with him, but August nearly ripped his throat out," I confirmed.

Above us, a door crashed open violently.

I kept my expression innocent, though something told me it was the door to my temporary room.

"Should we ask about that?" Miles checked.

"Probably not." My voice was cheerful, and I was trying almost as hard as Zander not to laugh.

"Why does Bash hate Anthony?" Tatum looked at Rafael as we headed up the stairs.

"They got in a fight at Miles and Zander's mating celebration."

Well, I hadn't known that bit.

"What kind of fight?" Miles knew as much about it as I did, apparently.

"A fist fight. Anthony's right arm took three weeks to heal," Rafe explained. For a supernatural, that was a long time. "He's not in our business. Bash could've killed the guy without much effort."

"What was Bash's reasoning?" Tatum asked.

Rafael shrugged.

Zander coughed again.

"I'd guess it had something to do with the staring," Miles said, studying me.

Bash stood at the doorway of the room that I assumed was mine, his arms folded and his gaze dark. "Gash here thinks he's my newest brother," I said calmly, giving him a friendly pat on the arm as I walked past.

He growled at me, but I ignored him.

Zander coughed again at my nickname.

"What has she done to him?" Tatum murmured to Miles.

"I have no idea," Miles whispered back. "How much longer until the girls' night?"

"Too long."

Bash stepped inside my room and closed the door behind me. His eyes were still narrowed.

"You said you'd stop glaring at me." I grabbed my suitcase, unzipping it and kneeling in front of it. I'd worn sweats and a tee for the flight, but they obviously wouldn't do for a dinner where I was supposed to be playing on Bash's possessiveness.

"You planned this with my mom."

"I didn't, actually. This was all her idea." I pushed hair behind my ear. "I didn't know he was coming until you did."

"He's not going to touch you." Bash's words were harsh.

"I never said he was."

"You've been looking for a hookup since August came into town, Brynlee."

"Thanks for making me sound so shallow," I drawled.

"That's not what I was saying." His voice was... frustrated. "We're sharing this room."

I sat up straight, my back still facing him. "We're *what?*"

"Sharing this room. I don't trust him in the same house as you, and I'm not snuggling with him."

"Well you're not snuggling with me either, *friend*," I shot back. "Your mom said there's an open couch. You can sleep there. I don't cuddle with my friends."

"I've seen you cuddle with Tatum and Miles on at least half a dozen occasions." His growl was back.

I hated how much I loved it.

"That's different. They're my sisters, and they've never watched me orgasm. If you want boyfriend privileges, you have to be my boyfriend. Right now, we're only friends in a way that benefits *you.*"

He was silent for a moment.

The door opened and closed behind me, then suddenly, I was alone.

I squeezed my eyes shut, dropping my head against the bed and letting out a long sigh.

My seduction plan sucked.

It took so much effort.

Why couldn't he just make it easy for me, for five minutes?

Granted, he had just offered a way to make it easier for me, and I'd turned him down.

But that was different, wasn't it? He wasn't offering to make my life easier, or to make me happy. He was insisting because he thought he needed it.

Anastasia's wicked plan was working against me, too.

A few minutes passed before someone knocked on the door. "Are you in there, B?" Miles called out.

Tears welled in my eyes.

Maybe I just needed to talk to someone.

"Yeah. You can come in."

Tatum and Miles slipped inside the room, locking it behind them.

"That doesn't look very comfortable," Tatum remarked. I was still on the floor in front of the bed, with my face against the side of it.

"It's not." I heaved a sigh. "I don't know what to do."

"Want to cancel the girls' night we have on the schedule and tell us what's going on?" Miles asked.

I lifted my watery eyes to her, widening them like I was shocked. "You would cancel something? What did Zander do to you?"

"You'd probably be disgusted if I told you."

Tatum snorted.

I laughed.

"Don't change the subject, B."

"I know. I'm just... It's weird. You're going to judge me."

They both gave me looks that said I was insane.

We never judged each other. Not rudely, at least.

"Fine. Remember how I thought Sebastian hated me? And how he'd never look at me, and made it a habit to never be where I was if he could avoid it?"

Both of them nodded.

"Well, he doesn't hate me. Mostly. Actually, maybe he still does. Anyway, what I'm trying to say is, I'm his potential mate. Anastasia figured it out after he chased me to a night-club and ripped me out from beneath a vampire's teeth. That's a long story. But yeah, he's obsessed with me. He also sort of hates me and doesn't want to be with me. I've been trying to seduce him into changing his mind. So basically, it's a mess," I finished.

Miles blinked.

Tatum blinked twice.

"Let's get the long version of that story, maybe?" Tatum finally said, looking at Miles.

Miles nodded vigorously. "We're going to need the long version."

I sighed, but launched into it anyway.

When I was done telling the story, they pulled me into their arms and squeezed me tightly. My tears had dried up, but I was still unsure of what to do.

"You and Anastasia are right," Tatum said bluntly. "Bash is a stubborn bastard. If he's not going to claim you on his own, you have to push him until he changes his mind. If he doesn't change his mind, you walk away. I'll help you do it, too."

My throat swelled. "You don't think I'm insane?"

"Of course not." Miles scowled at me. "You're potential mates. He needs to decide he wants you, or walk away. You're being a hell of a lot nicer about it than I would be."

I nodded, biting my lip. "So what do I do?"

"You hold your ground. He either wants to be your boyfriend, or he doesn't. Making him decide that isn't forcing him to be your mate. It's forcing him to decide what he's willing to lose. If he's willing to lose you, he doesn't deserve you," Tatum said.

I nodded again.

They were right.

I let out a long breath and wiped my face. "Guess I'd better get ready for dinner."

Miley smiled.

Tatum grinned.

Bash either wanted more with me, or he didn't. We were potential mates, and had been *just friends* for long enough.

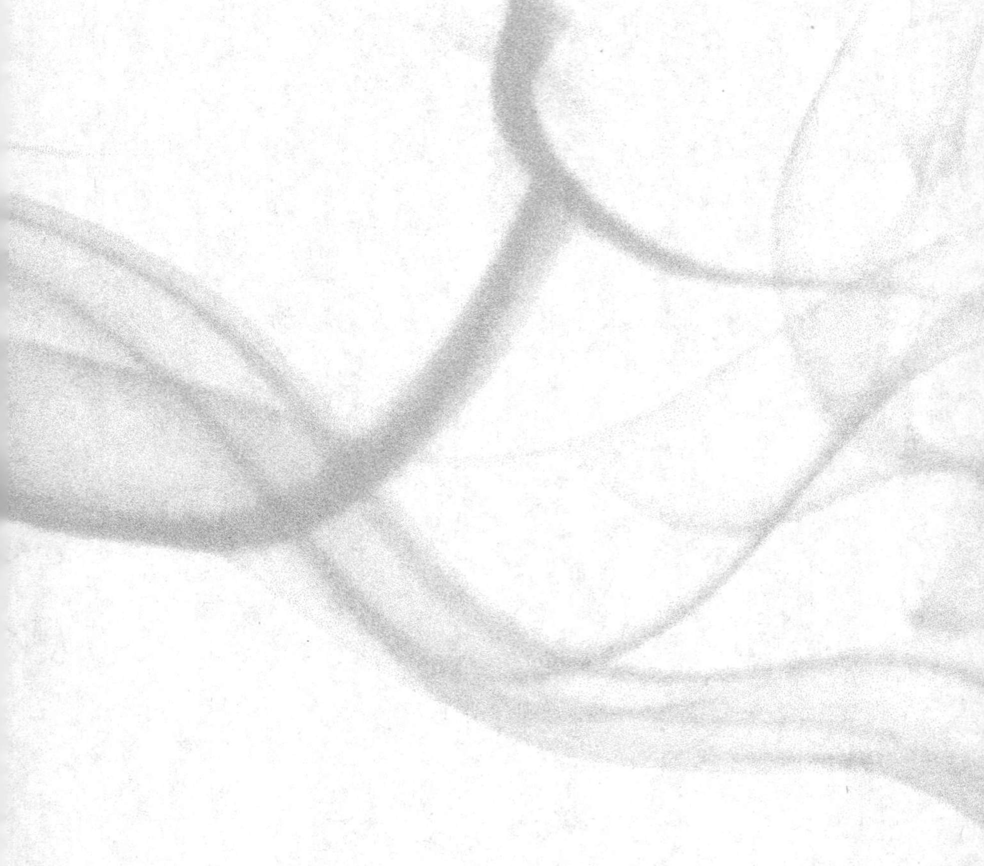

BASH

I JOGGED DOWN THE SIDEWALK, knowing I looked absolutely insane, but not giving a shit for once in my life. The rain had started pouring down, and every inch of me was soaked.

My hair was a mess.

My suit was askew.

Hell, my tie was even coming undone.

Brynn was already destroying me, and we were only *friends*.

Her words ran through my mind on repeat.

If you want boyfriend privileges, you have to be my boyfriend.

Right now, we're only friends in a way that benefits you.

I ran faster.

Pushed myself harder, too.

Our agreement had been fair, hadn't it? I'd regretted sending the message about watching her climax up until she agreed to my terms, but she *had* agreed.

And time-wise, the trade-off seemed fair.

Plus, I'd offered just to cook for her in exchange for chocolate. She had turned me down.

But physically, I could see the imbalance.

I watched her unravel every night. I didn't see her bare—didn't get to watch her fill herself with my vibrator, the way I wanted to—but she was vulnerable with me in a way I wasn't with her.

She didn't watch me climax with her name on my lips.

She didn't watch me stroke myself with her cries in my ears.

She didn't get any part of me, the way she shared herself.

If you want boyfriend privileges, you have to be my boyfriend.

Right now, we're only friends in a way that benefits you.

I hadn't asked what she wanted from me when we were establishing our friendship, either. I had decided on meals, just like I'd decided on chocolate and watching her every night.

She gave me my way without complaint, or request.

But had she wanted any of it?

Frustration had me slowing down to a walk, dragging a hand through my dripping hair.

I looked like shit, but I felt worse.

If you want boyfriend privileges, you have to be my boyfriend.

Right now, we're only friends in a way that benefits you.

I'd been selfish with her, and kept her at arm's length at the same time.

I'd hurt her *again*.

She deserved someone who treated her far better than I ever could.

But I couldn't let her go, so I had to figure out how to *be* him.

"Fucking hell," I muttered under my breath.

I didn't know how to be a boyfriend.

So I did what any sane, rational man would do:

I called my mother for advice.

"Hello," she sang into the phone. "Where did you run off to? Those didn't look like the proper shoes for the hour-long walk you've been out on."

"Don't make me regret calling you," I grumbled. "I need help."

She paused. "Did someone try to jump you in the street or something?"

I scoffed. "Who do you think I am, woman? If someone tried to jump me, they'd be dead. I need help with *Brynn*. And not the misguided kind of help where you invite fucking *Anthony* to Thanksgiving."

"I have no idea what you're talking about. I would never do anything like that."

"I'm serious. I need you to tell me what to do here, and not from the perspective of wanting me bonded."

She sighed. "Fine. What's the issue?"

"Long story short, I fucked up. She needs more from me, and wants me to act like a boyfriend. I have no idea how to be a boyfriend."

There was a moment of silence.

"Hello?" I grumbled.

"I'm here. Just processing this incredible news."

I groaned.

She laughed. "I've been mated a long time. I don't know how human labels work. If you want to know how to be a good boyfriend to her, why don't you ask her? Brynn isn't someone who'll be shy about sharing things like that. She'll tell you what she wants from you."

I pinched the bridge of my nose. "That's not very helpful."

"The most important part of any relationship is communication, Bash. If you can't communicate, you can't last. If you can't have an honest conversation with her about what she wants from you, you need to let her go."

"That's not an option." My words were a growl.

"Then neither is avoiding the conversation. Think about what you already know about her. Come up with a genuine way to apologize, to show her you mean it, then *talk* to her."

I let out a long breath. "Alright. Thanks, I guess."

"You *guess*?" she teased.

I massaged my temple. "Yes, I *guess*."

"Do you need a ride back?"

"No. If Anthony gets there, just keep the fucker away from my mate. If he touches her, you'll have to explain to the government how you got your nephew murdered."

"Mate? What happened to girlfriend?" she teased.

"You're a pain in my ass," I grumbled.

"Right back at you."

I ended the call, scheduled a car to pick me up, and wracked my brain for ideas as far as an apology went.

I hadn't talked to Brynn nearly enough. I hadn't asked her about her past, or what was important to her.

But she had mentioned *one* thing... and I'd use whatever the hell I could.

BRYNN

"HEY, ANTHONY." I slipped my hands in the pockets of my soft, gray sweater dress, flashing him my biggest smile. He looked a lot like the Villins, but he was related on Anastasia's side of the family, so his last name was something else. He'd told me at the mating celebration, but I couldn't remember.

Talking to Tatum and Miles had made me feel better about everything, but I really didn't want to test Sebastian on the whole, *"I will kill him if he touches you,"* bit.

Even though he was still missing.

Anastasia had promised he'd be back for dinner, but it was about that time, and he was nowhere to be found. I probably should've texted him to see if he was okay, but considering how he'd left, I didn't get the impression he wanted to talk to me.

I *had* left his bag in my room, though.

It was probably just me being too hopeful, but... well, I *was* hopeful. I wanted him to apologize, or at least just agree to try being more than what we already were. I was tired of what we were.

"Hey, Beautiful." Anthony stepped closer.

I stepped back.

The last thing I needed was for Bash to show up even *slightly* apologetic and find Anthony touching me.

"It's so good to have you here." Anastasia smiled, wrapping her arm around my waist and pulling me to her side. It was a hug, but also, a good way to keep Anthony away.

He grinned, dipping his chin a bit. "Where's Sebastian?"

"Oh, he's on his way. Had some work to take care of, but I'm sure he'll be here any minute," she said.

He chuckled. "That bastard is always working."

"Well, the real estate won't buy itself." She winked at him, and Anthony grinned. "Come here, I'll show you to your seat." She let go of me, and led him over to a seat. It had definitely held Sebastian's place card in front of it an hour earlier, when I first went down to check out the kitchen.

Bash and I had been seated on opposite sides of the table before, with me and Anthony sitting across from each other. That was part of Anastasia's plan, I assumed, and hadn't dared move the cards.

It *had* seemed a little too wicked, even for my taste. But we were at her house, so she got to make the rules.

It was probably better for everyone that she'd decided to switch the cards, though. Me and Anthony in particular.

"Food's here," Eldrich called from the kitchen, where he was pulling to-go boxes out of bags, and carrying the boxes to the table without missing a beat. We'd all given our orders an hour earlier, so hopefully he or Anastasia had ordered something for Bash.

Maybe I should've taken care of that.

Then again, we were just friends. And *barely* friends, at that.

"Come on, B." Miles waved me to the table, where she was already sitting in her chair on one side of mine. Tatum plopped down in the other, and both of their mates headed to the kitchen to grab the rest of the boxes for their dad.

I was on my way to the table when the door opened behind me.

Sebastian's presence was so strong, I could almost feel him.

I glanced over my shoulder, my heart stumbling when I saw the massive bouquet of red roses in his hand.

My gaze lifted to the rest of him, and my damn heart tripped again.

He was drenched. His hair was soaked, falling in messy waves all over the place. He tossed his suitcoat over the back of the couch, wearing his white shirt unbuttoned and the sleeves rolled up his forearms. His tie was nowhere to be found.

And those roses…

There were a lot of them.

"Flowers mean a guy is serious," I'd told him.

If they were for his mom, it would be a clear sign that I needed to kick his stuff out of my bedroom and make him spend an awkward night in bed with his cousin, or an uncomfortable one on the couch.

But he didn't carry them over to her.

He walked them right up to me, put them in my arms, and took my face in his hands.

His lips met mine, and it wasn't harsh or rough—but it wasn't soft and sweet, either.

It was confident.

It was possessive.

It was *hot*.

And it ended far too soon, when he released my face and slid an arm around my waist.

I was too dazed to respond properly, whatever *properly* was in that situation.

Every eye in the room was trained on us.

Most of their expressions were some shade of shocked.

Except Anastasia's. She was smirking.

Bash led me to my chair, sat me down in the seat, and pushed it in. He took the roses from my arms, smoothly carried them into the kitchen, and had them set in a vase of water less than a minute later.

Then, he took the seat across from mine.

His legs brushed mine, and I jerked away from the cold, damp fabric.

"You're freezing," I mouthed.

"Sorry," he mouthed back, though his lips were curved upward just slightly.

Everyone was still staring at us.

"Let's eat, shall we?" Anastasia's voice was cheerful as she broke the silence.

"Weather's great, huh, Bash?" Rafael drawled.

Tatum snorted, and her mate flashed her a grin.

Sebastian ignored him, taking a bite of his food instead.

"How are the new shops doing?" Eldrich asked Miles, further easing the awkwardness.

"Better than I expected," Miles admitted.

"They're crushing it. She's just too modest to admit it," I countered. "The locations in Wolfcrest and Wildwood have gone insane. I'm barely running any ads for them, and the shops are still a madhouse."

"They don't have any competition in those cities yet," Miles pointed out.

"It's not too late for Bash to kill *Sweet Dreams*," Rafael said.

"It's not," he agreed.

I kicked his leg, and his gaze lifted to me.

I narrowed my eyes at him.

"It is," he grumbled.

"Now that Brynn's poached their biggest customer, they might not survive anyway," Tatum said. "Let's not kick Cindy when she's already down."

"Who was their biggest customer?" Eldrich asked, his forehead knitting.

Bash stabbed another bite of his food as almost every eye at the table went to him.

Almost, meaning Anthony was too busy looking down at his plate, bored.

"Tell me it wasn't Bash," Anastasia said.

Bash took another bite.

"It was Bash," I said.

It was his turn to narrow his eyes at me.

"Why the hell were you their biggest customer? Everyone knows how much we hate Cindy. Or her actions, at the very least." Anastasia shot back. "Were you *sleeping* with her?"

"He wasn't sleeping with her. No one told him about the drama, so he didn't know he should avoid them instead of me. He tried to shut their business down after he found out, so he's already been forgiven, and he has a better chocolate supplier now."

"Hopefully one he pays very well in apology," his mother said.

"He does."

Miles' eyes cut to me.

She was my accountant, and therefore the only one at the table other than Bash that knew he didn't actually pay me for the chocolate. It seemed like a conclusion everyone could reach on their own, though.

When my gaze met Bash's again, his eyes weren't narrowed anymore.

There was *gratitude* in them.

Eldrich, the saint he was, changed the subject to seasonal recipes. Tatum could talk about the possibilities for at least an hour—and everyone else's contributions could make it two.

When Bash's cold, wet slacks brushed my legs again, I bumped his calf with my foot to tell him I appreciated the contact.

But I withdrew it before I got *too* cold, of course.

. . .

AFTER DINNER, Bash grabbed the vase of roses, took my hand, and towed me up to our room. He didn't say goodnight to everyone, so I figured he wasn't planning on holding me hostage all night.

Not *yet*, at least.

He locked the door behind himself, and set the vase on the dresser.

When he started undoing the rest of the buttons on his shirt, my gaze was glued to his forearms.

They were nice forearms.

Really nice forearms.

"I should be asking you what the hell the roses and kiss were for," I said, my eyes lingering on those damn arms.

"The roses were an apology. The kiss was a statement."

I scowled, finally meeting his eyes again. They were already trained on me. "You can't just hand me roses and kiss me like nothing's wrong when we're fighting, Trash. You called me a shallow slut, and said you didn't trust me to keep it in my pants while Anthony was here."

"Those were not my words," he growled. "And let's not use that particular nickname, shall we?"

He was right.

The *Trash* thing was a shitty move. I was just mad, and couldn't resist.

"Sorry."

"It's fine. I deserved it. Not again, though?"

I nodded. "Back to the argument, Brash."

"That one, I kind of like. It's not as good as Smash, though."

A snort escaped me. "Stop. I'm mad at you."

"As you have a right to be. But we both know I didn't call you a *shallow slut*, or say I didn't trust you not to jump on Anthony's dick."

"That was my translation, actually."

"Then you should rewire your translator." His neutrality was back, but I found myself not minding it that much. It was almost... dry.

Maybe a little sarcastic.

I could work with dry and sarcastic.

He tugged his shirt off, tossing it into an empty laundry basket I hadn't noticed inside the bathroom. Though I tried not to drool at all those gorgeous muscles, I definitely failed.

I'd never seen him shirtless before, but holy shit, it was a sight I could get used to. I had to shove my hands in my dress's pockets to stop myself from reaching out and touching him.

"I said you've been looking for a hookup since August moved in with you. That's the truth. I wasn't suggesting you were shallow—it's not shallow to want sex. If it is, I'm far worse than you at this point. I've been fucking my fist to a mental image of you for much longer than you've been itching for a hookup."

Heat rolled through my body. "I hope you haven't been using a *mental image* since you asked me to leave my door open."

His eyes moved slowly down my figure. "Definitely not."

Good.

"Turn around, Brynlee."

My forehead creased.

He spun his finger, and I understood what he was asking.

I turned around slowly.

When I faced him again, the bulge in his pants was bigger. "Damn, that dress."

"You also said you didn't trust me in the same house as Anthony."

"I don't trust *him*. He's hated me since we were kids. He'll do whatever it takes to seduce you, now that I've so loudly claimed you as mine. He'll lie. He'll mislead. He'll bring up old shit."

"I'll handle it, then."

"No, *I* will handle it. By not letting you out of my sight."

"You're going to have to let me out of your sight, because you're sleeping on the couch," I said bluntly.

"We're sharing the bed." He unbuttoned his slacks, and my gaze fixated on his erection. The slacks slid down, and his boxer-briefs hid almost nothing from me.

Shit, he was gorgeous.

I wanted him, *badly*.

He inhaled. "Your lust smells incredible."

My face flushed pink. "*Stop*, Splash. We're having a conversation. And we are not sharing the bed. I told you, you don't get boyfriend privileges when we're barely friends."

He strode into the bathroom and turned the shower on. I stopped breathing entirely for a moment, when he stepped out of his boxer-briefs. His back was to me, though it wasn't his *back* my eyes were glued to.

His ass.

Holy hell, his ass.

"I've decided I'm your boyfriend," he said stepping into the shower without turning back toward me. It was a walk-in shower with a solid stone wall between us, so I couldn't see any more of him.

Or his perfect backside, unfortunately.

It took a solid minute for my mind to process what he'd said after he stripped.

"Wait, what? You can't just *decide* you're my boyfriend. That's not how it works."

"Why not?"

I couldn't see him, but I could imagine his hands moving over his thick, corded muscles. Sliding over his ass. His cock.

Was it getting hot?

It had to be getting hot.

"Because dating implies that both parties get to decide. You can *ask* me to be your girlfriend. I can say no."

"Why would you say no? We're potential mates, Brynlee. You're already mine."

"I'm *not* already yours. I told you, I belong to myself. And as I also told you, our current relationship doesn't benefit me the way it benefits you. You feed me because you want to, and you stay with me at all times because you promised my brother you'd be his replacement. I—"

"I know." His interruption made me pause.

"You know?"

"Yes, I know. You deserve more." He stepped out of the shower, grabbing a towel off a hook on the wall.

My heart dropped into my stomach—or hell, maybe my vagina—at the sight of him entirely naked.

He was perfect.

So insanely perfect.

Thick muscle, everywhere.

Massive cock, hard and proud.

And that ass…

"You—what?" The words came out strangled.

He dried himself off way too quickly for my taste, then wrapped the towel around his hips, covering the goods.

"I know our friendship has been one-sided. I'm going to fix that."

"How?"

"I was planning on asking you that question, actually." He unzipped his suitcase.

It would be a shame for him to cover all that gorgeous muscle in a stuffy, boring, expensive suit.

"You can't just get naked in front of me like this," I found myself saying.

"You answered your door naked while we were still friends. We're dating, now."

"I still haven't agreed to that."

"I agreed for you." He dropped his towel.

My eyes went back to his ass. I tried to close them, but failed horribly.

"I won't date someone if sex isn't on the table. You said it's not. So, we can't date," I said, still staring at his butt.

"I said I was going to fix it."

"You're going to *fix* my needs?" The sarcasm hit, hard.

He stepped into a pair of boxer briefs, followed by a pair of slacks. "I've had sex with humans before, Brynlee. I can resist feeding. It's not easy, but I can manage. So yes, I'll fix it."

Anger flooded me. "I don't want to have sex with someone who looks at sleeping with me as a chore to be handled, Sash. I'm not a problem to be fixed. Sleep on the damn couch." I crossed the room, intending to open the door and gesture for him to leave.

His hand landed on my wrist before I reached it.

With one motion, he spun me toward him. My chest nearly bumped into his, but I stopped myself a few inches from him.

"Rewire your translator," he repeated, lowering my hand to his erection.

My heart lodged itself in my throat when he wrapped my hand around his cock, over the fabric of his boxer-briefs. It throbbed in my hand, and my body flushed.

"You keep assuming the worst of me. Stop. I'm talking about fixing the imbalance between us, not fixing *you*. I know you won't date me without sex on the table."

"You literally just said you could *manage* having sex with me. That it's not easy, but you can handle it. You need to rewire *your* translator." I tried to let go of his erection, but his hand tightened around mine.

His cock throbbed harder, and I flushed more.

"That's not what I meant," he said.

"Exactly."

His chest rumbled unhappily, but he was silent for a moment before he said, "I can manage having sex with you without giving in to the instinct to feed. It won't be easy to resist drinking your lust, but it's worth the effort, and I can handle it."

"That's slightly better." My anger faded a little as he spoke, though I still didn't feel desired.

His cock throbbed in my hand again, harder.

I squeezed it in response, and he grunted. "Careful, Brynlee."

"You're the one who said you're my boyfriend." I squeezed again for emphasis, and his eyes closed briefly.

"My family's downstairs. Your friends, too."

"So?"

"So, I'm not having sex with you for the first time when they could hear you. You may not have noticed, but you're loud when you get off."

"The insults just keep coming, don't they?" I drawled.

His eyes jerked open, narrowing at me again. "That wasn't an insult."

"Sure it wasn't."

His eyes narrowed further. "What do you mean by that?"

"I mean, you obviously don't like what you see or hear when I'm getting off. If you did, you'd come into my room or get involved," I bit out. "You've been watching me climax from the doorway without saying a word. You don't even ask me to strip."

"I thought that would be overstepping."

"And asking me to leave my door open while I use my vibrator every night *wasn't* overstepping?"

His hands caught my face, and he tilted my head back so he could look me in the eyes. His gaze searched mine. "You think I don't want you?"

"I think you don't want me anywhere near as much as I want you."

"Fuck that," he growled.

I blinked.

Before I could respond, he'd lifted me off my feet and was hauling me to the bed. My ass met the edge, and his massive hands shoved my dress up my body, exposing my thighs, then my thong.

The thin lace was on the floor a heartbeat later.

He opened my legs a heartbeat after that, and leaned in, inhaling at my core.

My entire body shuddered at the sight of him between my legs.

"Your scent makes me so hungry, I can hardly breathe, let alone think of anything else." He ran his nose over my clit.

I sucked in a breath, my hips moving a little.

His hands parted my legs more, opening me wider to him.

"The lust *blazes* off your skin. It should look like smoke, but yours is like fire. Burning for me. Pulling me in. Warming every damn inch of me. It takes everything I have not to drink it in, every time. If one of us wants the other more, it's me. Every minute of every day, it's me."

He finally licked my clit, and I barely clenched my jaw fast enough to muffle my noise of pleasure.

Hot.

Wet.

Firm.

His tongue felt *incredible*.

He grabbed a pillow off the bed. "Bite, Brynlee. No one but me gets to hear you." The words were so insanely possessive, my head spun.

I bit down on the pillow just in time for him to lick me again.

And again.

And again.

It only took a few strokes of his tongue on my clit before I unraveled on his mouth, crying into the pillow as my hips rocked and my body jerked.

"Fuck, your pleasure tastes good," Bash growled, his tongue slipping into my channel for a moment, licking more of me. "You're going to give me another orgasm before I let you back downstairs."

I moaned into the pillow.

His tongue found my clit again, and his fingers dug roughly into my thighs as he fucked me with his mouth.

The second orgasm hit almost as quickly as the first. I collapsed on the bed after riding it out, expecting him to release me.

Instead, he filled me with his tongue, licking more of my pleasure.

I cried out against the pillow, and my thighs gripped his head, trapping him against me.

His chest rumbled, his hands holding my thighs just as hard as they held him, but he didn't pull them off.

He just licked me until he'd had his fill, then opened my legs and slid free.

My chest was rising and falling rapidly. My hair was a mess, and my dress was still wrapped around my hips.

Bash took my panties off the ground, tucking them in the pocket of his slacks.

"I need those," I said, still catching my breath.

"You don't. I'll be eating you again when we're done with whatever my mother has planned for tonight." He rolled my dress back into place, tugging it as far down my thighs as it would go.

"I'm not *that* needy."

"I am." The words were blunt.

And holy shit, they made me hot.

"You belong to me, Brynlee. Don't forget it." He stood, grabbing a clean, white shirt from his suitcase. He had it buttoned up soon enough, but I put a hand on his when he reached for his suitcoat.

"Forget the coat. It's sexy when you roll the sleeves up. No tie, either."

He studied me for a moment.

I lifted my hand, leaving him free to do whatever he decided to.

A moment passed, but he left the coat.

And rolled the sleeves up to his forearms.

My body warmed, and his eyes moved over my skin.

Over my lust, if I had to guess.

"Would what we just did have sated you, if you were drinking from me?" I asked, as he stepped into the bathroom to fix his hair.

Eventually, I'd talk him into trying sweats and leaving his waves a little looser. We weren't there yet, but hey, baby steps.

"If I was feeding from you, we would've just been getting started."

The words thrilled me.

Maybe my seduction plan had worked after all.

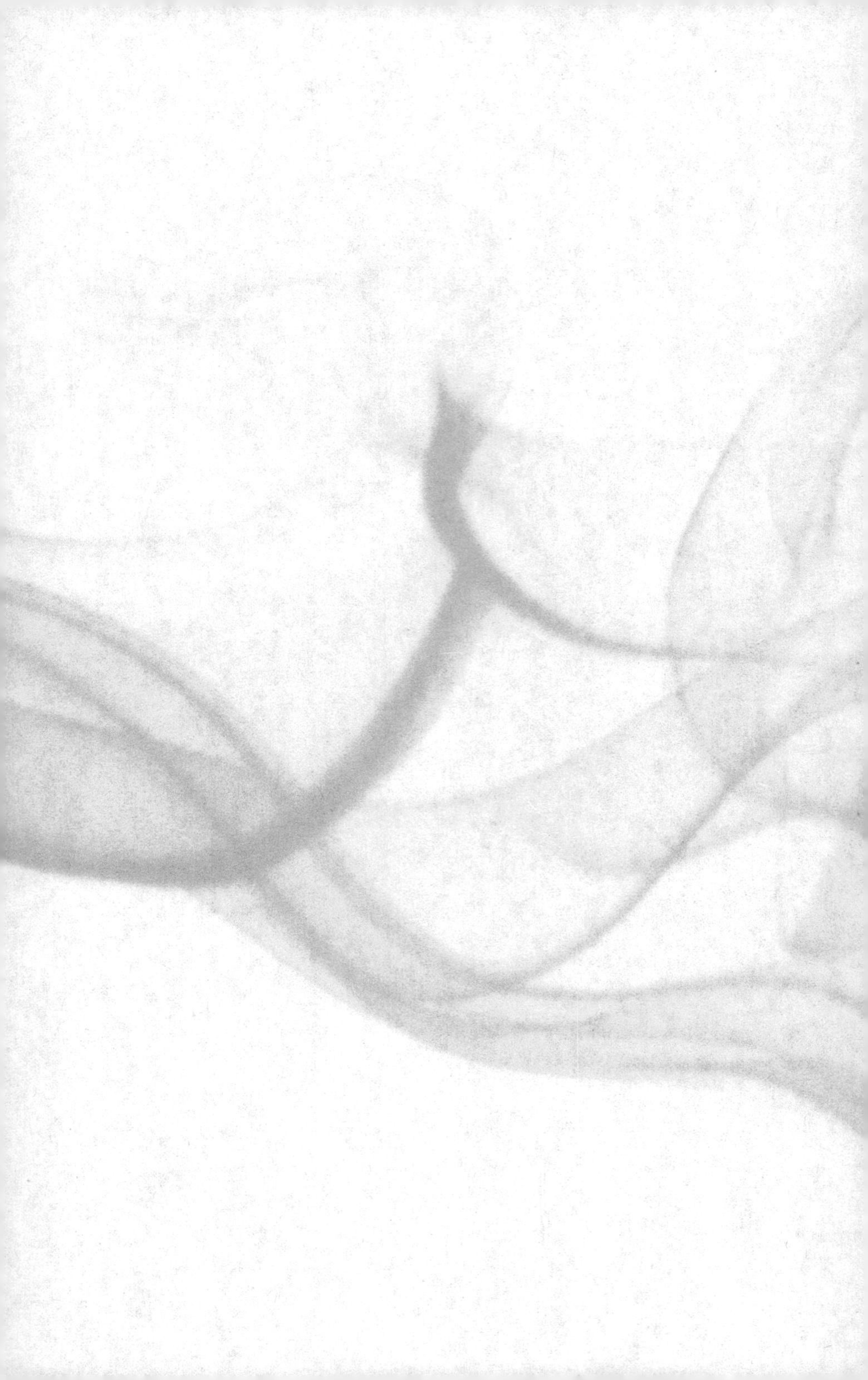

thirteen

BRYNN

WE WERE ALL UP LATE PLAYING cards and chatting. As Bash expected, Anthony spent much of the night trying to hit on me.

After his third attempt, Bash pulled me onto his lap, sitting me on his thigh. Since I had no panties on, my bare core brushed the fabric of his pants a few times.

Every damn demon in the room had to be able to see the lust on my skin and the pink on my cheeks, but thankfully, no one commented on it.

Anastasia beamed all night, though.

When we finally made it back upstairs, Bash barely waited until the door was shut before pushing me against the wood and kneeling at my feet. He shoved my dress up my thighs, and a breath later, was devouring my clit.

He unbuttoned his shirt while I clenched my jaw, my body rocking with his motions, and growled at me to bite down on the fabric before he refocused on my core.

His mouth was incredible.

Three orgasms later, he was tucking me into bed with him. He didn't have a shirt on, but his slacks had stayed.

"How do you feel about being woken up with my tongue on you?" His voice was low. I was still drenched between my thighs, thanks to the combination of my body and his mouth, and a bit dazed.

"Any time. Always," I whispered back.

His chest rumbled. "I want you out of this dress."

"Help me get it off, then."

He rumbled again, his hands smoothly peeling the fabric over my head. He pulled my hair out from beneath me, tucking me against him, my back to his front. His erection was stone against my ass, but he didn't ask me to take care of it.

I opened my mouth to offer, but was so tired, I forgot what I was going to say before I had the chance to say it.

A MOAN FLOODED THE ROOM, hot pleasure rolling through my body. My hips rocked, my body arched, and I could feel myself on the verge of an orgasm.

"Bite this," a gorgeous, low voice commanded, before fabric filled my mouth.

I bit down.

The wet heat flooded my clit again, and my body moved of its own volition, chasing the orgasm with everything I had.

The pressure increased until I was crying out around the fabric, intense pleasure flooding every inch of me.

Hot hands moved over my thighs, dragging against my clit. When they slid up my abdomen, I wrestled my eyes open, panting around whatever was in my mouth.

Bash's hot, blue eyes were on my breasts, his hands sliding over my belly, neck, and arms, touching every inch of exposed skin. I was still wearing my bra, so he left my breasts alone.

"Holy hell," I mumbled around the fabric.

He pulled it from my mouth, and I breathed in clean air.

"Good morning." His rumble was soft, but his gaze was still flaming.

"No kidding." I closed my eyes, ignoring the throbbing in my lower half.

"I want this gone." His fingers tugged on the cups of my bra.

"Take it off, then," I mumbled.

His hands were beneath my back, unclipping it before I even finished talking. They were full of my tits a moment later, and he squeezed them.

"You like that?" I whispered.

"You have no idea." His cock throbbed against my side, and I brushed my hand over it.

He swore under his breath. "Careful, Brynlee."

"Why should I be careful?" I struggled with the button on his slacks, but it finally popped free. "And why didn't you sleep just as naked as me?"

"I'm still fixing the imbalance." His voice was rough as I ran my hand over the front of his boxer-briefs.

"It's fixed."

"It's not—" He cut himself off with a hiss when I slipped my hand beneath the waistband of his pants, and wrapped it around the hot steel of his erection. "Fuck me."

"I was planning on it." I dragged my hand over him lightly, and he throbbed hard. "Think I can get you off as fast as you got me off, Slash?"

"Brynlee..."

"Mmhm?" I slid further down the bed, lifting his hands from my breasts to my hair. They sank into the strands, tangling and gripping hard.

"You don't have to—" His words became strangled when I dragged my tongue over the underside of him. "*Fuck.*"

"Feels good?" I wrapped my lips around the head of his cock, and met his gaze.

He throbbed, hard.

"Too good." His grip on my hair tightened enough that I couldn't forget he was holding me, but not hard enough that it hurt.

I sucked lightly, and he swore again.

I bobbed over his length, and his grip on my hair tightened again.

He was trying to take control.

The man was always trying to take control. I usually didn't mind it, but if I didn't set some ground rules, he would walk all over me.

And obviously, I wasn't going to let that happen.

I slid my mouth off him and met his gaze again, my lips brushing the head of his cock as I spoke. I was quiet, knowing he didn't want the whole house hearing us. They'd probably heard my moan already, but it was too late to worry about that. "If you want to finish in my mouth, you let me set the pace. Got it?"

A vein in his forehead pulsed.

His head jerked just a little.

He didn't want to give me control.

"You can feed from me if you ever decide you're willing to risk getting addicted," I added. "It wouldn't bother me."

His eyes closed.

That vein bulged a little more.

"You can't tell me that." His voice strained a little.

I loved the strain.

"That you can feed?"

"No. Tell me not to. I don't want to connect us that way."

That stung.

"I'm not going to say that, Nash." My voice was soft.

Though my body was still hot, his words had toned my desire down a little.

His jaw clenched tighter, his eyes still closed.

"Do you—" I started, but felt... *something*.

A pull of some kind.

My body relaxed, and every ounce of desire slowly slipped away.

I lowered my face to Bash's thigh, blissful numbness overtaking every ounce of lust, worry, sadness, fear... well, everything.

Bash's eyes opened.

The man was roaring a heartbeat later, flying across the room and ripping the door open.

I was too blissed-out to do anything but tilt my head a little so I could follow his movements.

His fist slammed into Anthony's face once, then again, and again.

Someone yelled something.

Sebastian snarled something back.

Zander and Rafe pried Bash off Anthony.

Eldrich dragged Anthony's limp body down the hallway.

Someone closed the door to my room, and I shut my eyes.

A nap sounded awesome, actually.

"BRYNN." Miley's voice was light as she shook my shoulder. I forced my eyes open, still a little numb. "Hey, how are you feeling?"

"So calm." I closed my eyes again.

"Sorry, but we need you. Bash lost his mind a little. Anastasia thinks you can fix him."

I yawned. "He'll be okay. He's Bash."

"Not this time, B. Come on. We need to grab you some clothes, too."

Tatum slipped into the room, looking right at Miles. "How is she?"

"Fine. Help me get her dressed."

I yawned again. "Just let me sleep."

"Bash needs you, B." Tatum's voice was just as light as Miley's, but there was a crease between her eyes.

She was worried.

She dug around in my suitcase, then abandoned it and grabbed Bash's button-up shirt off the ground.

"Do you remember exactly what happened?" Miles asked me, as she and Tatum slid my arms into the shirt.

"He said he didn't want to drink from me when I was giving him a blowjob. It hurt, but the pain vanished with the lust," I murmured. My eyes closed again.

Miley poked me in the side, hard, and I made a noise of complaint.

"No sleeping, Brynn. We need you to calm Bash down," she said.

I sighed.

Tatum finished doing up all the buttons, then stepped back and surveyed my appearance. She grimaced, but I didn't care how bad I looked.

"Just grab the suitcoat too and call it good. And get Bash some pants."

Something stirred inside me.

Jealousy?

"I'll get them." The words slipped out quickly.

Both girls looked at me, surprised.

I wasn't a jealous person, but I didn't want to think about one of my best friends carrying Sebastian's clothes.

My movements were slow as I bent down to grab his boxer-briefs, followed by his pants. My legs felt a bit shaky when I stood again, too.

"Where is he?" I still felt neutral, but there was a tiny bit of that *something* I'd felt a moment earlier. What little of it there was, was geared toward Bash.

"In the basement," Tatum said, grimacing again.

I blinked. "I didn't know there was a basement."

"There is. The guys used to keep violent vampires here while they gathered evidence against them," Miles said, helping me into Bash's suitcoat. "Anastasia would conveniently go out of town. Eldrich would stay and help as long as he could before the bond started to drive them mad."

"Huh," I said.

"I know you're wiped, but try to prepare yourself. Bash is pretty bad right now. I've never seen a demon lose control like this," Tatum warned me, as they led me out of the room. "Anastasia is barely keeping her shit together, and she always has it together."

"I heard that," Anastasia said from the living room, where she was pacing the grand space.

She wore a pair of silk pajamas, and her hair still looked perfect, but there were lines on her face I'd definitely never seen before. Her feet were bare, too, and I noticed a few splotches of what looked like blood on her shirt.

"Sorry," Tatum apologized quickly.

"It's fine. It's true." She ran a hand over her hair, and it immediately fell back into place.

"Is Anthony dead?" I asked. My voice sounded as neutral in my ears as Sebastian's usually did.

"Not yet," Anastasia said. "But he will be soon."

I stopped in my tracks, forcing Tatum and Miles to stop with me. "Why?"

"He fed from another demon's mate without permission. Your bond isn't sealed, but you were in bed together. All of us saw Bash claim you yesterday, so the violation is a grave one. Unbiased members of the supernatural government are on their way here right now, to make the ruling. They'll side with us, but we can't let Anthony die until they do," she explained.

Her expression was dark, and... sad.

The *something* inside me grew a little.

I decided it was my emotions making a comeback.

A roar below us made my head turn toward an open door that I remembered being locked the night before.

"Help him," Anastasia said, her voice edging on desperate.

If the supernatural government was coming, we needed to get Sebastian back to his normal self sooner, rather than later.

"How long until they get here?" I asked.

"An hour. Maybe two."

So I had an hour to get Bash back to normal. I wouldn't know how difficult that was going to be until I saw him, though.

"I better go," I said, heading toward the stairs. My knees were still shaking a little, my legs wobbly.

"I'll help you down," Miles said, ducking beneath my arm again.

"You'll stay right where I left you, Sweetheart," Zander countered, meeting us at the top of the stairs. He had a few bleeding gashes, and more than a few patches of blood on his bare chest and arms. The patches looked to be in various stages of drying.

Miley grimaced and nodded. "Help her, but let go before Bash sees."

Zander brushed a kiss to the top of her hair before grabbing my elbow. "Easy, Brynn. The last thing we need is for him to find you more damaged than he left you."

"I'm not damaged."

"You're not lusty, and you're typically lusty. That's a sign of damage for a demon. Bash will notice." Zander walked down the stairs with me, his grip on my elbow keeping me steady.

He released me before we reached the bottom steps, and stayed behind me as I carefully made my way down the last few.

When I stepped forward enough to see Bash, I froze.

My heart stopped.

He was in his demon form, with gorgeous, purple wings spread out behind him. Dark horns spiraled from his head, and magical tattoos moved over every visible inch of his skin.

He was *stunning*.

I'd never seen him in that form before, so it was new to me, but he was perfect.

His gaze snapped to me, eyes glowing bright red and chest heaving. Looking closer, I saw chains around his wrists and ankles, holding him in place. His hands were covered in blood, and he was cut up even worse than Zander.

"What did you do to him?" I asked, my emotions finally returning with a little more force.

"Stopped him from killing our cousin and earning himself a death sentence in the process," Zander said. "Supernaturals can't kill each other without consequences. If the government doesn't approve the murder, it's punishable by death."

Rafael spoke up from where he leaned against the wall. I hadn't noticed him, but he was close to the stairs, likely guarding them in his typical, casual way. Eldrich was beside him, a little less relaxed. "Bash isn't home right now. Our minds always get a little beastly when we shift, but this is something else altogether. What you see is the basest form of a demon."

"How do I help him?" I whispered.

Eldrich's expression was grim. "He can't hurt you because of your connection. You can try talking to him and touching him. If that doesn't work, you're going to have to feed him."

"I can't. He doesn't want to get addicted to me."

"If the options are addiction or death, we make that choice for him," Eldrich said. "Him losing control like this puts demons as a whole at risk. The government will understand his fury—but he needs to retain his sanity."

My throat swelled. "I can't force him to drink from me. He'll hate me."

"Talking and touching might work," Zander said lightly.

He didn't sound convinced.

When I looked back at Bash, I found his eyes still glued to me. His expression was angry, but I trusted he wouldn't hurt me.

"We'll stay to make sure you're safe," Rafael added.

I nodded, then made my way across the basement. The floor was concrete, and cold beneath my bare feet. My legs didn't shake as much as they had before, though.

"Hey, Clash," I murmured, approaching him slowly. I was safe with him, but that didn't mean I wanted to startle him. "It's me."

His chest rumbled at the sound of my voice, and he fought violently against his restraints. Blood ran down his arms, and a panicked cry escaped me. My gaze jerked to Eldrich and the other guys. "Let him down."

All three of them shook their heads together.

I rushed forward, throwing my arms around his middle. My face met his bare chest, and my eyes stung at the feel of blood on my skin. Maybe I shouldn't have, but I hoped it wasn't his.

He continued fighting, his face twisted in a snarl as he tried to hold me.

"Give him his arms," I commanded, lifting a watery glare to his family members. "The bindings on his legs will keep him here."

The guys exchanged a look.

"*Now!*"

Sebastian went still against me when he heard the tone of my voice.

"Don't move while they release your arms," I ordered the demon, my grip on his middle still tight. "And don't hurt them. They're mated. They don't want me."

Bash's body was tenser than I'd ever felt it, but he remained completely still while his father unlocked one of his wrists, followed by the other.

The moment his dad stepped away, he hauled me into his arms and buried his face in my neck, inhaling my scent. His hands moved roughly over my skin, making sure I wasn't hurt anywhere.

"No one touched me," I said, forcing my voice to stay authoritative since he'd responded well to that. "I'm fine. I need you to shift back, Stash."

He ignored me, just holding me tight and breathing me in. One of his thick arms snaked around my ass, holding his shirt and suitcoat down to cover my backside.

I gave him a few minutes to cool off, remaining where I was. Though I kept hoping he would decide to shift back on his own, he didn't.

"Shift, Bash," I commanded. His real nickname felt weird on my lips, since he'd never given me permission to use it.

He didn't budge.

I turned my head, looking back at his dad and brothers.

"We don't have much time," Eldrich warned. "He needs to look sane. That means showering, patching his wounds, and getting dressed."

Shit.

I'd used at least five minutes of our potential hour already; maybe ten.

And I definitely wasn't horny.

How was I supposed to *get* horny, though? With Bash not sane, while knowing he was going to hate me for feeding him, even though it was likely the only way to keep him alive...

The situation wasn't exactly a turn-on.

"Try the tail or the tips of the horns," Rafael advised, gesturing above his own head.

My face flushed.

Demons had more erogenous zones than humans. I knew that.

"I'm setting an alarm for thirty minutes," Eldrich said, holding up his phone. "We'll be back when it goes off, unless you call us down sooner."

"We'll close the door. Basement's soundproof," Zander added, already heading up the stairs.

Rafe and Eldrich followed him, and the door closed a moment later.

"It's just us now," I said quietly, burying my fingers in the messy strands of Bash's hair. There was blood in it, but I didn't let myself think about that. "I need you to touch me."

I didn't want to play with his horns without having a conversation about that. He didn't even want to feed from me, so I was pretty sure his demon form would be off limits.

His chest rumbled, and the arm he had around my ass vanished. A moment later, his hand slid up my thigh and between my folds.

I sucked in a breath at the touch, tightening my grip on his hair.

His cock throbbed against my hip, so much thicker in his demonic form, but he just touched me.

Something sharp dragged over my ass lightly then slapped it, harder. My hips arched, my gaze jerking over my shoulder.

His tail.

He'd spanked me with his tail.

If it wasn't so hot, and his hands weren't working my clit like they were made for me, I would've laughed.

My desire swelled instead. "Are you hungry, Sebastian?" I breathed.

He rumbled more violently, two of his fingers slamming into my channel roughly.

I choked on the words I'd been about to say, his thumb working my clit so hard I lost control. My cries flooded the room as I rode his fingers, climaxing hard and fast.

"Do you even want me?" My voice was shaky, and I tried to regain control of myself.

"More than I want to keep breathing." The words were snarled, but they were there.

"Prove it, Bash. Feed from me."

He roared, and there was so much emotion in it, my eyes stung.

I hadn't wanted to force him.

I hadn't wanted to steal his freedom.

To seduce him, yes, but never to take away his choices.

His lips parted as he inhaled deeply, and he staggered backward. The massive, steady, controlled demon *staggered*.

His back hit the wall with a heavy thud.

His fingers curled inside me, and my body arched.

He breathed in again, and again, filling himself with my lust.

More cries escaped me as he dragged his thumb over my clit, *hard*.

He drank, and drank, as he dragged me back to the edge until I shattered.

Again, and again, he fed on my pleasure and made me climax. Distantly, I heard an alarm go off.

Some part of me knew that meant we were running out of time.

"Sebastian," I panted, burying my fingers in his hair and forcing his gaze up to mine. It was insanely hot—and insanely hungry. "We have to stop. Your government is coming. They're going to kill you if you can't look sane again."

He took in another inhale of my lust.

"You have to shift," I said, using my grip on his hair to shake his head. "Come on, Smash. Shift."

He inhaled again, but his fingers finally slid out from inside me.

I unwrapped my legs from around his waist, but he didn't lower my feet back to the ground.

"Shift, Crash." I tugged on his hair one last time.

Finally, his body shimmered.

Those gorgeous wings vanished.

The back of his hornless-head met the wall. His eyes slammed shut, his breathing rough and his grip on my body still tight.

It had worked.

But what was I supposed to do after it had?

Bash would want space. He'd been very clear about not wanting to get addicted to my lust, and I'd given him no choice in the matter.

What if he would rather let his government kill him?

I eased my feet to the floor, and he let them go.

The basement door opened above us. "Brynn?" Eldrich called out.

He'd undoubtedly been elected the interrupter.

"We're fine. He shifted back. Just a second," I replied.

Bash opened his eyes, and they were blue.

I'd forgotten how pretty they were.

"I'm sorry," I said quietly. "Your family said there was no other choice. I wasn't trying to take your freedom."

He didn't say anything.

I didn't really think there was anything to say.

I stepped back, grabbing his pants and boxer-briefs from where I'd dropped them on the floor earlier. "Here. I'm sorry."

Sebastian accepted the clothing, but his attention moved to his dad and brothers when they came back down the stairs. I slipped away while they freed him from the last of his restraints and filled him in on what was going to happen.

The other guys must've told Tatum and Miles what I'd said about Bash hating me for feeding him, because they immediately pulled me into their arms.

"Thank you." Anastasia's words were thick, and genuine. "I'm so sorry. I should've known better than to push him like that. I should've realized Anthony might try something worse than flirtation."

"You didn't know what would happen. I didn't, either. We learned our lesson," I said quietly, wiping away a few tears that had escaped and looking at my best friends. "Can I stay with one of you guys until we head home? I can make the floor work for one night. I just need to shower really fast."

"Zander will take the couch." Miles squeezed me lightly.

"He can crash with Raf in my bed," Tatum said. "The three of us can snuggle. It'll be just like old times."

My smile was a little watery, and I didn't feel it at all, but it was the best I could offer given the situation.

They helped me collect my stuff and get it all back to Miley's room before I slipped into the shower and finally let the tears fall.

fourteen

BASH

I SAT with my back to the wall and my head resting against the cement. My gaze lingered on the empty, concrete space in front of me.

"You need to shower and get dressed," Rafael said, for the third time. "You need to be ready when they get here."

I heard him, but the words didn't register.

My body was too quiet.

My mind was too clear.

My muscles had never felt so loose before, despite the pain in my balls from the lack of release.

I didn't give a damn about the pain.

My hunger was *gone*.

My brothers grabbed me by the arms and heaved me up off the ground. I grunted at them, but it was half-hearted.

I could breathe fully, without pain.

I was... at peace.

Rafe turned the shower on, and they dropped me beneath the water. It was cold, but I didn't mind. The whole damn world looked different without the ache of hunger cutting through me.

"Where's Brynn?" I asked.

"Getting ready to talk to the government, like you should be," Rafael said. "Wash your damn hair. We're running out of time."

"Who's with her?"

"Tatum and Miles. She's fine," Zander said.

I'd need to see that for myself, so I finally grabbed the soap.

"They're here." Rafe swore. "Mom will buy us a few minutes. Hurry up."

I did as he said, though I still felt so at ease, there was no stress behind the actions.

Two minutes later, Rafe was buttoning one of my shirts over my chest while Zander dried my hair with a towel. I was still too calm to care.

"What the hell is wrong with you?" Rafael growled. "Your life is on the line here."

"I'm not hungry," I said.

"Welcome to mated life," Zander abandoned his efforts to dry my hair. He grabbed my suitcoat, instead.

"I've never not been hungry."

"It'll pass, and you'll want her naked again in an hour," Rafe said, reaching for my tie.

I already wanted her naked again. The lack of hunger was just a newer sensation.

"No coat." I stopped Zander. Brynn preferred it when I rolled my sleeves up and ditched the coat.

"You're bleeding through your shirt in a dozen places. The coat goes on." Rafael grabbed it from Zander. "You won't get to fuck her again if they kill you."

I hadn't fucked her in the first place.

That would change as soon as possible.

"They won't kill me. Any mated demon would do exactly what I did if someone drank from their mate." My shoulders tightened at the memory.

And Anthony was still alive?

"*We* know that. But you need to be your normal, uptight self so the government doesn't use this as an opportunity to take one of us out," Rafe said.

"We've got to go." Zander opened the door.

Buttoning my coat to hide a spot of blood I'd noticed on my abdomen, I followed him out. I didn't give a damn about my messy hair, or my lack of shoes.

At the bottom of the stairs, I found Brynn already sitting on the couch. Her soft, golden hair was damp, and she had on a simple, light pink sweater dress that clung to her gorgeous curves. Tatum and Miles sat on either side of her as she finished telling her story to the supernatural government's representatives. She'd left out all the details about the sex, thankfully.

I recognized both of them immediately. Ronin was a werewolf, and Maggie was a vampire. Neither of them had anything against us. She was mated, and while he wasn't, the wolves were a hell of a lot more possessive over their mates than demons.

My life definitely wasn't at risk.

I walked around to the front of the couch, and picked Brynn up without pause. She made a noise of surprise, but didn't protest as I sat back down with her on my lap, her back to my chest.

Tatum and Miles slipped away, giving us space as I told my side of the story, and we both answered their questions. Soon enough, they'd agreed it was my right to end Anthony's life if I chose to do so, and walked out of the house.

Brynn slipped off my lap, forcing a smile. "Good acting, Crash."

Good *what*?

I blinked, and she was already disappearing up the stairs. Miles and Tatum followed her, and I rose to my feet, intent on doing the same.

Zander and Rafael stepped in front of the stairs, blocking my path.

"What the hell?" Irritation colored my voice.

"Sorry, we've got strict orders to give the ladies their space," Rafael drawled.

"Come help me cook," our mother called from the kitchen.

None of us budged.

"My mate is upset about something. I'm going to talk to her. Move, or I'll move you," I said.

"We know why she's upset." My dad draped an arm over my shoulder. "We'll fill you in while we cook. Not much time left to get Thanksgiving dinner made."

I grumbled, but let him lead me to the kitchen.

Mom was putting the turkey in the oven, her expression grim. "We'll be eating late, this year."

"Don't stress about it, Love. No one minds." Dad released me, pulling her into his arms and plopping a kiss on her forehead.

Her lips curved upward the tiniest bit, and my chest ached.

I started to turn around, to go after Brynn, but Rafe and Zander immediately blocked my path again.

"What do you remember about being in the basement?" my dad asked, putting a recipe card in my hand. I didn't look down to read what it was for.

"Not much. It's a haze."

Anger, I remembered.

Fury.

A little pain, too.

Everything had gotten easier when Brynn wrapped her arms around me.

Her body had felt incredible on my fingers.

Her lust had made me feel so damn alive.

"She didn't want to feed you her lust. She said you didn't want to get addicted to her, and would hate her for forcing you," Dad said. "There was no other option. None of us could get you to shift back, including her. Drinking from her was the only way to snap you out of it. We made the decision for you; not her."

I blinked.

"She apologized to you multiple times after you let go of her down there," Zander said. "You didn't respond."

"I was dazed. I've never felt sated before," I growled back, shoving my way through my brothers. They didn't put up as much of a fight as I expected.

"Anthony's in your old room," Dad called over my shoulder.

I halted.

A new wave of fury hit me, *hard*.

I would deal with him.

Then, I would talk to my mate.

BRYNN

"WE SHOULD HELP ANASTASIA," I said, pacing Miles' room. "I think she's planning on doing a full Thanksgiving, even after everything."

"You wanted space from Bash," Miles reminded me.

"I don't know what I want, and I can't stay in this room all day." I raked a hand through my dampish hair. It was barely wet, but definitely not dry.

"This is probably the wrong time to tell you, but there's a pretty big blood spot above your ass," Tatum remarked.

I peered over my shoulder, trying to see the spot, but failed. It was too far down.

"I'll change, then we'll go help Anastasia," I decided.

My friends nodded.

A few minutes later, we were making our way down the stairs. My determination faded halfway down, when guilt clenched in my belly again.

I didn't want to face Sebastian.

It was too late to turn around, though.

Thankfully, when we got to the kitchen, Anastasia was in there alone.

"Did those bastards leave you to do everything yourself?" Tatum asked.

Anastasia flashed her a smile, though it didn't reach her eyes. She felt bad about everything.

So did I.

I would never let myself make another wicked plan again. Evil and I were clearly incompatible.

We all grabbed a recipe and got to work. Anastasia turned some Christmas music on to try to lift the mood while we cooked.

Tatum and Miles kept the conversation moving even though Anastasia and I didn't say a whole lot.

AN HOUR LATER, all four of the guys came in through the door, one after another. Bash was the last inside, and I turned away from him, squeezing my eyes shut and letting the stand mixer in front of me run longer than I probably should've.

The whipped cream was going to be *extra* whipped.

The mixer shut off, and a pair of massive hands landed on my hips.

I froze.

My eyes stayed shut.

Lips brushed my ear. "We need to talk, Brynlee."

Shit.

"I'm busy."

"It wasn't a request."

"We can talk later," I whispered.

"We can talk *now*." He dragged me back a few steps, and I had to open my eyes to see where I was going.

"Deal with the whipped cream, Rafe," Bash said. It wasn't an order... but it was.

Rafe saluted him as Bash continued walking me backward, until we were free of the kitchen and everyone in it. Then, he turned us both. His hands remained on my hips as he walked me toward the stairs, his front brushing my back as we moved.

A lump stayed in my throat all the way to the spare room that was intended to be mine, but only held Sebastian's things.

He sat me on the edge of the bed before he finally released my hips and stepped back. His gaze was intense, and moved over me slowly, as if he was making sure I was alright.

Or debating the best way to kill me.

Or maybe, trying to decide where he wanted to taste me next.

My cheeks pinkened at the idea, though I knew the first option was more likely than the latter two.

"You changed your dress," he said.

That was a much easier topic than the one I'd expected.

"There was blood on it."

His eyes narrowed.

"*Your* blood." I gestured toward his abdomen, where I could see a massive blood splotch on his white button-down, thanks to his suit being undone. He was probably bleeding in other places, too.

He didn't glance downward.

"Are you still bleeding?" I asked. It seemed like an easier conversation than the one I knew was still coming.

"No. We heal quickly, when we're fed properly."

And I'd fed him properly... I hoped.

I didn't say anything else.

I wasn't sure what else *to* say.

He'd made it clear that he would be pissed if he drank from me, and I made him drink from me anyway.

"You told my family I would hate you for feeding me," he said, eyes narrowing at me again. He was still standing in front of me, so damn tall he was way above me, and I was still on the bed.

"You made that much clear when we were in bed," I said.

His eyes narrowed further. "Like hell I did."

"You didn't want to connect us. You said addiction to me would be stealing your freedom. Most people would hate someone for taking away their free will."

"Adjust your damn wires, Brynlee. There's a huge difference between not wanting something, and hating someone for it. I don't want a pink t-shirt, but if you give me one for Christmas, you're not my enemy."

I knew he was talking about the translator thing again, and scoffed. "Adjust *your* wires. There's a huge difference between a pink shirt and a connection that would take a decade to break, Sebastian. Miles went through this—I know everyone else's lust will taste terrible to you for the next ten years because of what I did."

"I've wanted you so badly for the past year, everyone else's lust already tasted like shit to me," he growled. "And you don't use my full name."

"I've never been given permission to use your nickname," I tossed back.

"Why would my mate need to ask my permission to call me what she wanted?"

The question caught me off guard for a moment, but I recovered relatively fast. "I'm not your mate, Bash. What we have isn't permanent. I'm human, and I'm aging. You're not. What I want has never mattered to you. I'm sorry for going against your wishes when I fed you, and I think it's best that we start building the distance back up between us now."

I stood, but he put himself in front of me the moment I moved toward the door.

"You're not listening to me, Brynlee."

"And you're not listening to me!"

"Yes, I am." He stepped toward me.

I stepped back.

He took another step forward. "You're worried I'm angry about you feeding me. I'm not."

I stepped back again.

"You think the people who care about you are okay with letting you grow old and die alone. We're not." He moved forward again.

I tried to step away, but my back met a wall.

"You're afraid we're not permanent. We are." He stepped up close, his body pinning mine to the flat surface. I inhaled sharply, and his hands slid up the curve of my hips until they found my waist. I held my arms between us in an attempt to create distance.

"You can't guarantee that," I said, my heart beating rapidly.

"*Aeternum,* Brynlee. Tell me you're mine, and we'll seal the bond here and now."

"I can't do that. We're barely even friends," I whispered. "You're still angry that I fed you, and—"

I cut myself off when his hands caught my face and tilted my head back. "Look at me. Do I look angry?"

My throat swelled.

He didn't.

"I was trying to avoid the addiction for as long as I could, but I knew it was inevitable. I chose to open your thighs and taste you, knowing it would only be a matter of time until I lost control when I did. You fed me to save my life—that's a hell of a lot better than me eventually losing my grip on my hunger."

Tears welled in my eyes, and my fingers tightened on his suitcoat. "I felt like the devil, Bash. Everything that happened was my fault. Even in your demon form, I had to *seduce* you into drinking from me."

"My mind was controlled by my fury when I was in that form. I barely understood what was happening. It sure as hell isn't your fault that Anthony decided it was wise to drink from my mate. That was a decision he made entirely on his own."

"He was only here because your mom and I had an evil plan. I was supposed to use my body to convince you to mate with me. We realized it made more sense for me to turn into a demon than a vampire, and I told her I'd do whatever I could to break you. She invited Anthony to push you."

"Is that supposed to make me less attracted to you?" His thumb dragged over the single tear that had trailed down my cheek, wiping it away.

"I don't know. I never should've done it."

"Like hell you shouldn't have. You're my mate; if you want to tempt me by cooking in a thong and masturbating in the room across from mine, that's your right." He wiped away another tear, using his thumb again. "Anthony made his own choice. I fought the bastard before; he knew exactly what he was doing when he drank from you."

"I still feel awful about it."

He brushed a kiss to my lips, lightly. "I'm sorry."

"Well it's not *your* fault."

"If we're playing the blame game, the only reason he was here is because I refused to fuck you even when you were shaking your bare ass in my kitchen. If you had any idea the thoughts that were running through my mind..."

"Dirty ones?" My grip on his shirt tightened.

"Filthy. They'd make these cheeks so pink, the color might never fade."

My lips curved upward, just the tiniest bit. "I don't know, you said it had been ages since you touched a woman. I probably have a dirtier mind than you."

He chuckled, the sound low and rich. "Sure you do."

"Give me your number, then. How many women have you been with?"

"You don't want to play this game with me, Brynlee." He massaged the sides of my scalp lightly, not releasing his hold on my face. "You give me a number, and I'll turn it into a checklist of men to kill."

My face warmed. "That wasn't an answer, Bash."

"I've been with three humans before you. Only one of them, more than once. Half a dozen demons as well, though I haven't slept with one of them in a few decades."

My eyes rounded. "Only nine? You definitely don't want my list."

His chest rumbled. "I'll fuck you so many times, you won't remember anyone else."

"Is that a promise?"

"Yes." He lowered his lips to mine and kissed me lightly. "It's a request, too. Your lust sated me in ways I never imagined were possible. My body still feels more relaxed than ever."

"Are you hungry again already?" I asked, my heart warm.

"Only a little. Not nearly to the point I had accepted as my normal. It's barely noticeable at all."

"Good." I closed my eyes for a long moment.

"If it's any consolation, I fully support your choice of demonism over vampirism," he murmured, still rubbing my scalp lightly.

"I'm still going to become a vampire if you never decide to seal the mate bond," I said, my voice quiet.

"Brynlee, I tried to seal it a few minutes ago. *Aeternum.* Tell me you're mine, and the bond will be settled."

I shook my head lightly. "If I seal it now, you'll probably change your mind when we're back at your house. And besides, we're still barely friends. I hardly know anything about you."

"It's *our* house. And if you're refusing me now, it gives me the right to play just as dirty as you."

My eyes widened slightly. "What does that mean?"

He brushed his lips to mine again, the kiss still light. "You'll figure it out."

"Asshole."

He chuckled again, nipping at my ear before he released his hold on me. "We should go downstairs and see if we can help salvage the holiday."

I sighed.

"No guilt," he warned. "If I see you looking guilty, I'll drag you into the hall closet and feast on you until your guilt is gone."

My body warmed all over again—but when he towed me out of the room, I didn't put up a fight.

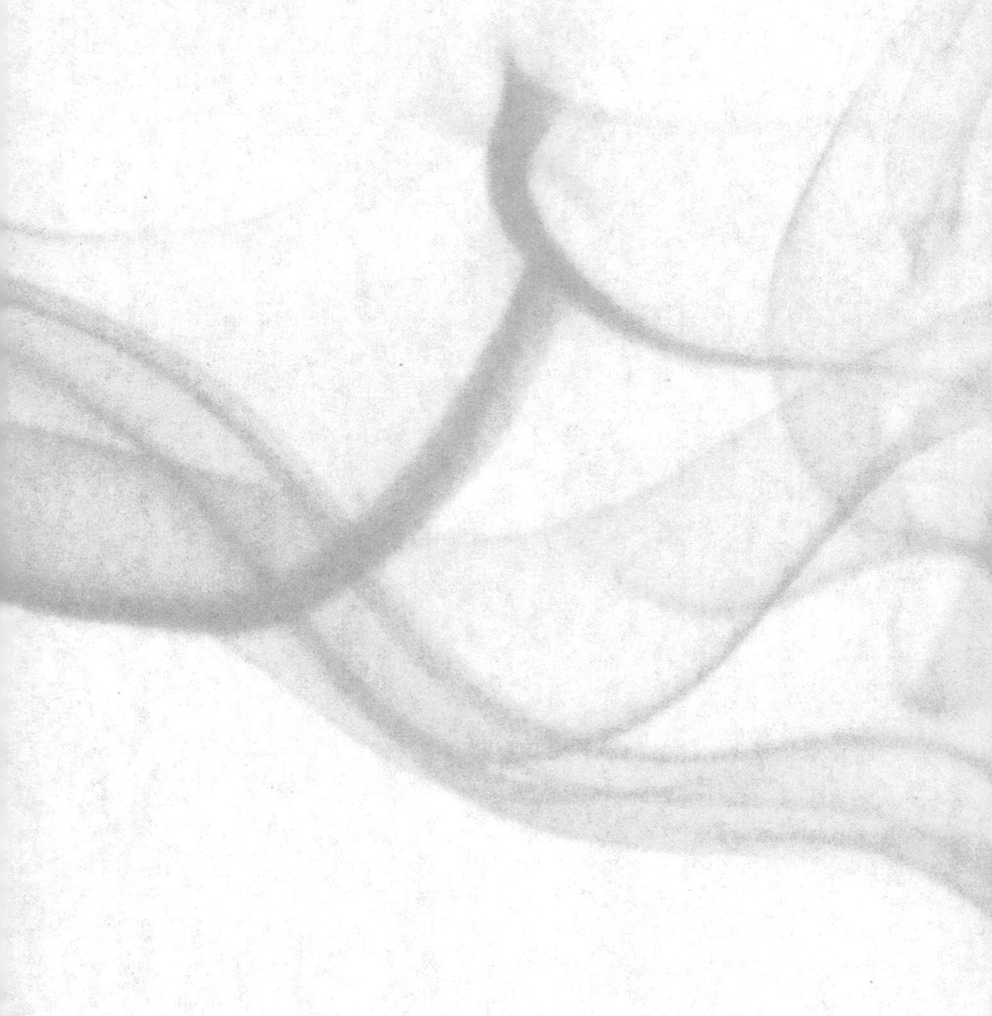

BRYNN

THANKS to the events of the morning and early afternoon, our timing was off for pretty much all of the Thanksgiving food. After a little debate, we all decided we'd rather eat everything as soon as it was ready.

We started eating in the middle of the afternoon, and didn't stop until nearly midnight, when the huge turkey was finally done.

I'd never felt so full in my life. And no—for once, that wasn't a sex joke.

Bash left me on the bed and carried my suitcase back into our room when we finally called it a night. I was sprawled on my back on the bed when he made it in, half-asleep already.

"You're not naked," he grumbled at me, dropping my suitcase next to his.

"I don't have energy for sex," I mumbled back.

"It doesn't take energy to let me get you off, Brynlee."

"It takes energy to get my clothes off, though."

Bash grabbed the hem of my dress and peeled the tight fabric up, then off of my body.

I groaned. "You're still hungry?"

"Mmhm." He unbuckled my bra and slipped it down my arms, freeing my breasts. He squeezed them, and my body warmed.

Maybe he was on to something when it came to letting him get me off.

"You have to touch yourself too, if you're going to touch me. I'm too tired," I mumbled.

"I don't have to get off." He dragged my thong down my ass. "And I thought we talked about you being done with panties."

"You talked about it, then stole my thong. I don't remember ever agreeing."

"You'll agree."

"Sure I will."

He dragged a finger over my clit, and I sucked in a breath.

Maybe I really *would* agree.

"You do have to get off, though. I'm not agreeing to this if you're not getting off too, and we both know you'll stop if I say no."

He growled at me. "I'm fine."

I reached over and dragged a hand against his erection through his slacks, making him clench his jaw.

He'd made me orgasm so many times, and I hadn't even taken care of him once. Our relationship was getting lopsided in *my* favor.

My hand moved over his hardness again.

Maybe I had enough energy for *something*.

"Drink my lust while I touch you," I said, rolling onto my side to get myself a little closer to him.

"Brynlee." His hot gaze was on my hands as I unbuttoned his pants and freed his cock. The way he looked at me warmed my body.

"How bad did your balls ache today?"

He didn't answer.

I squeezed the head of his cock, hard. "Bash."

"Fucking badly," he gritted out.

"You interrupted me earlier. Didn't even seem like you wanted to finish in my mouth," I countered, stroking him lightly with one hand while I pushed his pants down with the other. He shoved them down his thighs, lips twisting in a snarl and eyes closing when I stroked him a bit rougher.

His reaction to my touch was enough to make me hot.

"Of course I wanted to fill your mouth." His answer was harsh.

It made me wetter.

"Are you going to give me control?" I countered, dragging my tongue up his underside. His hips jerked so roughly, I had to grab the base of him just to hold on.

He swore in response.

"Tell me I'm in charge," I murmured, my lips brushing the head of his cock with the words.

It throbbed hard in my hand. "I wouldn't last long."

"Tell me, Bash."

"You're in charge, baby." I could tell it took him a hell of a lot of effort to say the words, and they made me hotter.

I lifted his hands to my hair, and they tangled in the strands like they had that morning. "Can you see how much I want you?"

"Of course." His grip tightened, borderline painful but not quite there yet.

"Drink it while I get you off."

"I can't, Brynn. I'll shift."

"Then shift." I wrapped my lips around his cock.

He swore again, loudly, and I handed him my bra. It was in his mouth a moment later, and I was sucking him.

I bobbed on his cock, and remained in place, his body tense but still for the most part. He'd agreed I was in charge, after all.

He was close—I could taste him, and knew he was. But he still hadn't drank from me.

My lips came off his erection with a soft popping noise. "*Drink*, Bash."

He shuddered, and his nostrils flared as he inhaled.

His body shifted, his wings unfolding behind him. My eyes widened as his cock swelled in front of me, thickening. It throbbed, and I knew he was going to lose it.

I had my lips around him in time for him to finish in my mouth, cock jerking with every spasm as he flooded my tongue with his taste. He was sweet—like the damn chocolate he ate so much of.

Something warm and hard slipped between my ass cheeks as I lost it, and I sucked in a breath as the tip of something almost *sharp* dragged over my opening, then my clit.

My thighs closed around it.

My gaze lifted to whatever it was, and widened when I saw his tail threading between my legs. Though my mouth was still wrapped around his cock, the throbbing of his climax had ended.

My entire body shuddered as his tail slid against me, back, and forth. Whatever was rubbing against me wasn't actually sharp—it just had a pointy end, and there were multiple of them. They felt triangular, with a point that hit me perfectly, curved just enough that it didn't hurt.

Supernatural guys could have multiple orgasms, so I knew Bash could keep going.

My hips rocked as I rode the ridges on his tail, the thick cord moving back and forth while I bobbed on Bash's erection.

He drank deep lungfuls of my lust, abandoning my bra to take more of me. His hips moved with my mouth, just a little, and I loved that he was letting me have my way with him.

His cock muffled my cries when I shattered on his tail, and his grip on my hair tightened when he throbbed again, flooding my mouth with his pleasure once more.

He eased me off his erection, then rolled me to my back and opened my thighs.

His eyes burned into me as he watched his tail work me, and he covered my mouth with his palm when I lost control again.

He inhaled my lust until I'd come down from the high, then tucked us under the blankets after he shifted back.

Bash's erection slid between my ass cheeks as he dragged my back flush against his chest, and my eyes closed as my lips curved in happiness.

"You taste incredible," he said into my ear, his arm tight around my waist. "Ready to seal the bond yet?"

I smiled wider. "I still barely know you."

"I like to cook, I eat a lot of chocolate, and I overthink every-thing," he said, nipping lightly at my ear.

My smile grew. "That's not exactly knowing your hopes and dreams. Or your history. We're still sticking with friendship for now."

He sighed. "I'll tell you what you want to know tomorrow."

"Mmhm." I wasn't convinced. It wasn't that I didn't believe him—it was just that he seemed pretty damn private, and I didn't think he would open up as easily as he said.

"That enough sex to take care of your needs?" he mumbled, sounding almost as tired as I felt.

"I haven't even had your cock yet."

He chuckled. "You're fucking perfect."

"Can I get another *baby*, then?"

"You're fucking perfect, baby." He brushed a kiss to my neck. "Go to sleep. We've got to leave in a few hours."

I fell asleep wearing a smile that wouldn't budge.

BASH'S ALARM woke us up way too soon, and we blearily joined my friends and their mates downstairs, waiting for the ride Bash had scheduled. It showed up right on time, and I tried to finger-comb my hair while we drove.

I'd ended up smooshed next to Miles and Zander in the back, but at least they were both sleeping. Tatum and Rafael were talking quietly, and one look at Bash told me he was annoyed.

I bit my lip and pulled up my messages.

ME

The back of your head looks grumpy

His head jerked toward me, and I met his gaze. His face softened, his attention moving over me before he looked back to his phone.

BASH

Next time, we get in before them so we can sit together

ME

Deal

I thought he'd leave the conversation like that, but another message came through a moment later.

BASH

Any plans for today, after we get back?

ME

Think I need to make another batch of chocolates

BASH

As long as you forget the panties this time

I sent him an eye-rolling gif.

BASH

I'd make it worth your time

ME

Idk if there's a way to make cooking in commando worth my time. The discomfort… shudder

BASH

There's nothing more comfortable than not wearing pants

ME

You only think that because you've never worn sweats in your life. Or maybe because you're made of muscle. All my skin rubs and gets sweaty. It's uncomfortable.

BASH

I like you sweaty

ME

You've never seen me sweaty, Smash

BASH

I can picture it. Believe me, I like you sweaty.

My face warmed.

ME

What did you picture?

BASH

Cook without panties on tonight, and I'll show you.

ME

You're trying to seduce me.

He glanced over his shoulder, undoubtedly checking to see how much lust was around me, before looking back.

BASH
And it's working

ME
There are better ways to seduce me.

BASH
Care to share?

I sent him a middle-finger gif, and he sent one back of someone licking a peeled banana.

I snorted.

ME
Is that supposed to be me?

BASH
That's me, licking your finger

ME
My finger is not banana-sized

BASH
My cock is a lot bigger than a banana, if that's what you're suggesting.

ME
Especially in your demon form. Hot damn. Didn't see that coming.

Pun totally intended BTW

BASH
You're clearly the one trying to seduce me, baby

ME

Finally, you realize

BASH

I should've asked about your obsession with cooking half-naked sooner, but I didn't want to jinx it or accidentally make you put on pants.

ME

You should've just grabbed my ass.

BASH

I should've bitten it.

He sent me a teeth emoji, and I sent back a devil one.

ME

My brothers are coming for Christmas and make-up Thanksgiving in a few weeks. We'll need to pretend we're not having sex. Assuming we're still having sex, at that point.

BASH

We will be having sex for the rest of our lives, Brynlee. I'm done pretending you're not my mate.

ME

They'll legitimately kill you.

BASH

It'll be amusing to watch them try

ME

They're DRAGONS.

BASH

I'm a DEMON.

ME

But have you ever seen a dragon? They're gigantic

BASH

Have you ever seen a dragon fight? They don't train.

ME

I guess...

I'll still worry for your life

BASH

Guess you'll have to seal the bond with me by Christmas. They won't try to kill me if our lives are connected.

ME

You haven't changed your mind yet?

BASH

I don't change my mind after it's made up. Ask any of my brothers, or their mates.

ME

You changed your mind about not wanting to be with me

BASH

I was fighting myself on that. It's different.

ME

Sure it is.

BASH

Should I send the licking gif again?

ME

If that's your way to convince me to suck you, it's not working

BASH

I haven't had to convince you thus far

ME

Asshole

BASH

I do intend to get acquainted with
yours, yes

Damn, I can taste your lust from up here

He breathed in lightly, not taking enough lust to force a shift, but definitely drinking from me.

My body flushed.

BASH

If me feeding from you turns you on, I
won't have to do much seducing, will I?

ME

Shut up

Bash sent me the damn banana gif again, and I couldn't help the snort that escaped me.

AFTER SOME TIME in the airport and a decently-long flight, we were finally back in the Hummer and driving home.

It felt good to be alone with Bash again, even though there was still uncertainty between us. At least, on my side of things. He seemed pretty certain.

Tatum sent a message in our best friends group chat as we all left the airport.

> **TATUM**
>
> Don't forget birth control, B. I'm not ready to be an aunt yet
>
> **MILES**
>
> Neither am I

I sent them the same middle finger gif I'd sent Bash.

> **ME**
>
> Pretty sure Bash is more child-opposed than either of you.
>
> **TATUM**
>
> Idk, I think he'd be a good dad
>
> **MILES**
>
> I think he'd freak out for a minute, but step up real fast. He'd probably put you on a healthy meal plan or something. No chocolate for you.
>
> **ME**
>
> I'm not getting pregnant, so it doesn't matter
>
> **TATUM**
>
> On second thought, I'm liking the idea of this. You know Anastasia's going to be all up in our grills for a baby after the last of her boys is mated. If B gets knocked up, it takes all the pressure off of us.
>
> **MILES**
>
> This is a valid point. Someone has to take the fall, and Brynn does want a big family

"Why did Rafael just text me that I need to knock you up as soon as our bond is sealed?" Bash asked me, and my head jerked toward him.

"What?" My face was hot. "Oh, that. Right. Tatum and Miles are trying to convince me that we need to have a kid after we seal the bond, so your mom doesn't start pestering them to do it. I mentioned wanting a big family at one point, so they've decided I need to take the fall for them."

"You want a big family?" Bash sounded surprised.

"Yeah. I have three brothers, and despite their recent over-protectiveness, I've always liked knowing I'm not alone."

He was quiet.

Really quiet.

"I'm not saying we would need to have a big family if we do decide to seal the bond," I added quickly. "I know it would be a decision I would make with my husband. Or mate. I—"

He set a hand on my thigh, and I cut myself off. "I haven't considered having kids for a long time. You caught me off guard, that's all. I honestly don't know how I feel about it."

I nodded, swallowing the lump in my throat and looking out the window.

I hadn't been prepared for how a mate bond would feel so... out of order. After growing up human, in my mind, the natural route was friendship, dating, engagement, then marriage.

Instead, ours had started with ignoring the bond, then refusing to act on it, to a weird sort of friendship, and to sex-friends. It was weird, and I didn't know exactly how to feel about it.

But that was life, I supposed.

And hey, I couldn't complain about the sex-friend bit.

seventeen

BRYNN

BASH CARRIED my suitcase upstairs for me, leaving it in my room and looking out at the space. His expression told me he was thinking *something*, but didn't give away any details.

I told him I was going to shower and change before cooking, and when I waved him out of the room, he didn't complain.

As I stepped into the bathroom, my phone vibrated with another text.

BASH

Running an errand. Be back soon. Don't leave without me.

ME

Do you realize the irony of leaving without me and telling me not to do the same?

Also, if you're meeting a woman, including Cindy, I will remove your wings from your body.

BASH

I'm not meeting a woman. How many
times do I need to tell you I'm yours?

ME

Then why do you need to go alone?

BASH

I called a place. They didn't answer. Want
to surprise you.

A surprise?

That was actually really sweet.

ME

Fine. Send me pics so I know you're not
secretly meeting someone.

A selfie of a very unamused Bash, sitting in the Hummer
again, came through immediately.

BASH

Happy?

ME

Tickled pink.

BASH

I'd like to tickle you pink

I snorted.

ME

What happened to neutral, boring
Sebastian?

BASH

He finally got his mouth on his mate's
body. No going back now.

I bit my lip to stop myself from grinning.

ME

Have fun on your errand. Don't touch any other women.

BASH

Don't touch yourself. You don't get to climax unless I'm there.

My body heated.

ME

What if I do?

BASH

I'll lock you in my house

ME

You already did that

BASH

Ha ha.

Touch yourself without me there to watch and I'll drink your lust for an hour tonight before I let you get off.

That was actually a pretty good threat.

I didn't doubt his ability to go through with it, either.

Deciding it would bug him the most if I just didn't answer his text, I set my phone on the counter face-down and slipped into the shower.

Honestly, I wasn't horny, and had no desire to pull out my vibrator. If he was gone for too long, I'd do it just to bug him. But, if I was going to get off, I might as well feed him when I did. Two birds with one stone and whatnot.

I didn't want him hungry, after all.

There were plenty of things I was unsure of, but that wasn't one.

I TOOK A LONG SHOWER, and when I dried off, found a dozen more selfies and messages from Bash. He hid where he was, but had texted me enough times that there was no doubt in my mind that he wasn't meeting anyone.

I'd been in bed with him. Nothing had distracted the man when we were together, except another guy drinking my lust. And that one was pretty much impossible to ignore, considering it had put an end to my side of our exchange.

More pictures came through while I got dressed and combed my hair. He'd asked me to make chocolate without panties on, but I was more interested in teasing him than giving him what he wanted.

When he didn't get what he wanted, he wanted more.

Then again, he also wanted more when he did get what he wanted.

Pros of being with a demon, I guess.

There were cons though, too. The long lifespan was one of them, because it meant things had happened that I didn't know about and likely couldn't imagine.

Things like him mentioning that he'd considered having kids at one point.

Which meant he'd had a lover in the past. One he was serious about, because Bash definitely didn't strike me as a man who would jump headfirst into single-fatherhood. He was a workaholic.

Thinking he'd had a human lover reminded me of our conversation about partners—and his admission that he'd been with one of the humans more than once.

Something told me it was a lot more than once.

My twisting stomach agreed.

I checked my phone after drying as much of my hair as was possible with a towel, and saw that Bash was already on his way home. Though I debated doing something freaky, like using my vibrator to catch him off guard when he got back, I was a little unsure about everything.

So, I left my panties on my bed and headed downstairs in nothing but my *Coffee & Toffee* tee.

He found me in the kitchen, gathering everything I needed for his favorite peppermint truffles.

I glanced over my shoulder, and raised my eyebrows when I saw four vases of red roses in his arms. "What are those for?"

"You." He set one down on the dining table, and another on the middle of the kitchen island before he stepped up behind me. "Flowers mean a guy is serious, after all."

Bash slid his free hand over my ass, chest rumbling in satisfaction when his fingers found my damp center, and he realized I wasn't wearing anything else. "I'll be right back." He disappeared up the stairs.

Something told me one or both of the other two were going in my room.

He was back in the kitchen a few minutes later, and his hands immediately found my ass, squeezing hard. "I've pictured burying myself inside you in this kitchen for so damn long, Brynlee." He parted my ass cheeks, and I grabbed the edge of the countertop, holding on for dear life. "Don't move."

He kneeled between my legs, turning, and I moaned when his mouth found my clit.

My body trembled as he slowly licked and nipped at me, dragging me toward the edge.

"We need to talk," I said, my voice breathly and my body shaking with need.

"Alright. Talk." He kept licking me.

"Have you ever been in a serious relationship before?" I managed to get out.

His tongue stopped.

I squeezed my eyes shut.

I'd seen that one coming.

"Why?" His teeth finally dragged over my clit, and I clenched my jaw to stop myself from crying out.

"You said you'd considered having kids before. You don't strike me as someone who would want that without a partner."

He was silent for a minute.

A long minute.

His tongue kept working my clit, and I couldn't stop my hips from rocking. My cries filled the kitchen as he made me climax, and he finally slipped out from between my legs, standing behind me.

His hands landed on my ass while I caught my breath. "Why does it matter?"

"You want us to be mates, Bash. Mates should know these things about each other."

He was quiet again.

"You don't have to tell me," I said, when he didn't speak up again after a while. My legs were still shaking, and his hands still felt incredible on my backside. "But I'm not comfortable with continuing the way we are if you can't trust me with your past. You asked me to be your mate—I expect you to back that up by acting like one."

"I'm not young, Brynn. I have a past," Bash finally said.

"I know. But I'm not comfortable sharing my life with someone who can't trust me with theirs." I looked back at my ingredients, starting on the recipe again.

A few minutes passed, and his hands finally left my ass.

More emotions welled in my throat as he left the kitchen, and I gave myself a minute to feel them.

Then, I focused on the task at hand:

Truffles.

When I was done with them, I would focus on my ads.

I FINISHED THE CHOCOLATE, wishing I'd worn my panties, but was too tired to work on my ads. I shuffled up to my room and closed the door behind me before collapsing against it, my eyes shut.

I opened them after a minute, and nearly screeched when I saw a massive, gorgeous man sprawled over my bed.

"What are you doing in here?" I demanded, my heart pounding rapidly.

"Waiting for you." Bash's head was propped up on his arm, and there was a sheet of paper on the bed beside him.

"I'm not having sex with you," I warned, staying where I was.

I was too easily distracted by his hands. And tail. And dick.

"That's not what I'm here for." He picked up the paper and held it out toward me.

Reluctantly, I crossed the room and took the paper without looking down at it. "What's this for?"

"You wanted the story. I figured you'd want a picture to go with it."

Oh.

Ohh.

I had the paper flipped over in a heartbeat, and my eyes moved hungrily over the image.

It was a picture of Bash sitting at a table in a restaurant, with one arm around a small, severe-looking woman. She had pale skin and dark hair, and wore glasses. Neither of them were smiling.

"I don't have any pictures of her on my phone or computer," Bash explained. "I had to dig into an old social media site to find it. She was human."

"*Was?*"

"She died a few years back. Her name was Carrie."

I stared down at the picture, trying to work it out in my mind—Bash, having feelings for a woman like the one in the picture. Her image didn't tell me a whole lot, obviously, but the fact that she wasn't smiling did.

"So this was just a few years ago?"

"No, it was a few decades ago. She was on one of Zander's tech teams while we were working on a rogue vampire outbreak. We met when I stopped in to grab something from Zander, and she asked me if I wanted to grab drinks after work. I never said yes to that shit, but for some reason, I did. We ended up in my hotel room, in bed together."

My stomach clenched.

Maybe I was more possessive than I thought.

"It was a long time ago," he repeated, eyeing me. "Are you sure you want this story?"

"Yes." I sat down on the edge of the bed, not entirely sure, despite what I'd just said.

He continued. "I didn't think it would happen again, but when she texted me, I gave in. I couldn't drink enough lust from her to keep the hunger at bay, because we weren't potential mates, but I'd never managed to keep it at bay anyway. We didn't do anything together outside the sex—it was just sex. But it mattered to me."

I could see where the story was going, and my heart hurt for Bash.

"After a few months, I invited her to spend a holiday with my family. The request shocked the hell out of her. She thought I was joking. She asked what I thought we were, and I told her I saw us as dating. She asked how I thought that would work, given my immortality."

He continued, "When I suggested she could eventually become a vampire so we could spend our lives together, she laughed. The next day, she was gone. Her stuff was out of her apartment, she'd given Zander her resignation, and taken her things from there, too. When I texted to make sure she hadn't been abducted, she called and told me she was fine. She'd resigned in person, and was posting pictures of herself in another state two days later."

"She wasn't interested in a serious relationship," I said quietly.

"No. It wasn't important to her. I saw it as something that would grow over time, that might lead to having kids, but she was only in it for the sex. That's all there is to it, Brynlee. I'm not trying to hide it from you. It's just awkward. I've never been good with women, and clearly, I'm shitty at relationships."

"You're not shitty with me."

He lifted an eyebrow, obviously disagreeing.

"I'm serious, Bash. You listen to me, well enough that you remembered my casual comment about how I feel about flowers. You take care of me first when we're together, whether sexually or just physically, with food. You make me smile. You make me laugh."

I set my hand on his thigh. "We're still trying to figure things out, but you're right—a relationship grows over time, as long as both people put effort in. I think we both are, even if most of my effort has been focused on trying to seduce you, and most of yours has been on trying to fight the bond."

He set his hand on top of mine. "I'm not fighting it anymore."

"Good." I hesitated, then added, "What was she like, personality-wise? From the pictures, she looks like my opposite."

He grimaced. "She was a lot like Miles. Anal. Organized. Particular. We were a terrible match. We disagreed constantly, and she wasn't playful like you are when shit hit the fan. She was... grumpy."

"So you were dating yourself in woman form," I said. "There was no sunshine to balance it out."

"Basically. It was a while before I could look back and realize how shitty we were together. It wasn't until you moved in that I realized why fate matched you and I."

"Why?"

He lifted my hand off his thigh and brushed a kiss to my knuckles. "Because you're fun, Brynlee. You wake me up. You make my life happier, and give it purpose. You find joy in everything, and when something happens, you roll with it. That's difficult for me."

"You rolled with me feeding you."

He chuckled. "I wanted that so damn much, it hurt constantly. It's not hard to accept getting what you want."

That was fair.

He kissed my knuckles. "It'll take me time to get used to opening up about shit like that. You'll have to push me sometimes, but I'm trying, Brynlee."

"I believe you." My words were honest. "And I'm pretty good at pushing you."

His lips curved upward. "It's a unique skill you possess."

"I know." I ruffled my hair with my free hand.

He dragged me across the bed until my hip met his, our bodies facing in opposite directions so we were looking toward each other. "I didn't explain myself well when it came to why I want the mate bond now. To me, the bond would be a starting point. It would change you, and give us both stability. We would promise each other our lives, then make it work."

"I have a hard time looking at it like anything other than marriage," I admitted. "And in my mind, you don't get married until after you have everything figured out and decided. I think I would feel different if any of my brothers were mated, but I only ever knew *of* mates—I never saw them together as a kid."

"Well, I can wait as long as I need to." He dragged his tongue lightly over my knuckles. "But I'll probably keep trying to convince you to seal the bond."

"That's alright. If you push me, I'll push back."

"Good." He pulled me close, resting his chin against my cheek as he held me in his arms. "I never realized how much I would enjoy cuddling."

"I definitely didn't see you as a cuddler," I agreed.

"You'll just have to put up with it, I guess."

"I also happen to love cuddling." I turned my head until our eyes met, then brushed my lips against his. "And kissing."

He captured my mouth, the kiss firm, but not rushed. Our tongues made love slowly, my body pressed up against his.

Bash rolled me on top of him, his hands gripping my ass while his mouth moved with mine. I parted my legs, straddling him despite the slacks he had on. His body rocked with mine, the movements smooth and slow.

When I pulled away, I was breathing fast.

He was too.

"Damn," I whispered.

"I want you, baby. All of you."

Finally.

"Take me, then."

Bash slipped my tee over my head before he dragged my lips back to his.

The kiss grew deeper, and it wasn't rough.

It wasn't brutal.

It felt like coming home.

…Pun not intended, but I'd take credit anyway.

He rolled me onto my back without breaking the kiss. My fingers popped the button on his slacks, and when I pushed them down, he helped me strip him.

My hands slid down his bare thighs, then up his ass.

Shit, his body was perfect.

I gripped the tight bubble of his backside while he dragged the head of his cock over my clit. I was wet, and he slid over it without a problem, making me gasp.

"You're not ready for me, are you?" His voice was low, the head of his cock still dragging over my clit.

"Like hell I'm not." I grabbed his hand, taking him to my entrance and moving my hips. I couldn't stop my moan when the head of his cock pushed into me, insanely thick and hot.

I'd missed cocks.

I'd definitely, definitely missed cocks.

My chest rose and fell rapidly as my body adjusted to the size of just his tip. It had been way too long.

Bash grabbed my thigh and opened me wider. "Ready for more?" His growl made me wetter.

"Stop asking. Take what you want, Bash."

He pushed my legs open wider, and thrust.

My head tilted back, my face twisting with the intensity of the sensations as he filled me completely.

Holy shit.

Holy shit.

Holy shit.

"That's a hell of a cock," I moaned, hips arching further.

He was hitting every spot I had.

Every.

Damn.

One.

He wasn't even moving, and I was so close to shattering, it wasn't even funny.

"It's yours, baby. The only one you'll ever feel from now on." He thrust again, and I screamed.

The climax hit me hard.

So insanely hard.

The orgasm felt endless.

In some corner of my mind, I noticed his snarl and the way he slammed into me, losing control inside me. It only dragged my pleasure out more.

I was moaning when I came down from the high. "Shift, Bash. I need you to shift."

"You're not ready." The hand holding him up moved over my breast, squeezing before it traveled down the curve of my hip, and caught my ass. "Fuck, I want to watch this bounce. Turn around."

"Shift, and I will."

"Not happening right now, baby. I have no desire to break you." He smacked my backside lightly, and thrust into me a few more times. "Turn around. Give me your ass."

I groaned, but followed his order. It took a little maneuvering to roll over without sliding off his cock, but the way he throbbed inside me told me he didn't find the awkward movements unsexy.

My ass was in the air a moment later, my cheek on the pillow. His hands gripped my ass, spreading me wide as he slid deeper inside me.

I couldn't help the cries that escaped me when he filled me.

And filled me.

And filled me.

My hips rocked.

Savage sounds escaped him, his fingers finding my clit as he moved us, giving me the rough, hard fuck I'd been waiting for.

I was screaming again in minutes, my channel strangling him. He climaxed with me, spanking my ass hard enough that it stung as he swore and flooded me with his release.

"Shit," I moaned, my hips still moving as the aftershocks rolled through me. "How are you so good at that?"

"I was made for you." His growl was possessive—and hot. "You good with the spanking?"

"So good with it. Go harder next time."

He gripped handfuls of my ass. "You're so fucking sexy, nestled up against my body like this."

"It's one of my best qualities." I wiggled against him, and he pumped into me a few times, making me want more.

Bash smacked my ass again, though it was playful and light. "Ready?"

"Hell yes."

His chest rumbled in satisfaction, and he drove into me, distracting both of us from our conversation.

The distraction went on for most of the night—and ended with both of us collapsed on my bed, sweaty, sticky, and insanely spent.

Bash pulled me into his arms and murmured, "*Aeternum, Brynlee.*"

My throat swelled, and I whispered, "Soon."

It was perfect.

Absolutely perfect.

And I didn't want to change a thing.

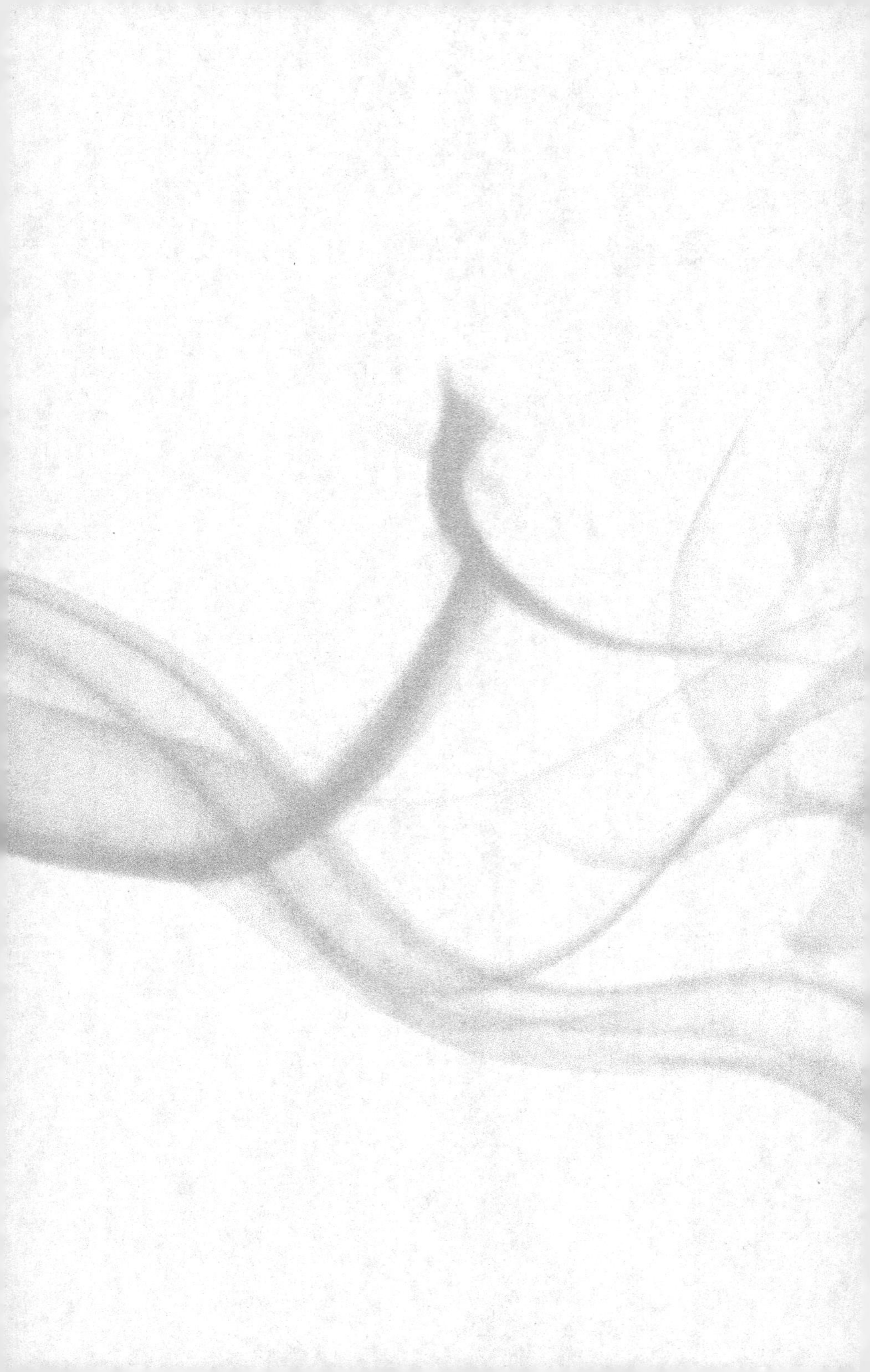

eighteen

BRYNN

THE NEXT FEW days passed by in a whirlwind of sex and work. When there wasn't sex or work, there was food.

And talking, too.

We worked on the couch or on one of our beds, so we could be close to each other.

I was making an effort to have conversations with Bash about my life, and he was doing the same. As much as I enjoyed the sex, the conversations were what made me feel good about our future.

He never shifted for me, or fed from me while he was inside me—the man was still too worried about hurting me—but that didn't make it any less hot for me.

Every night, he gave me a chance to seal the bond.

And every night, my "soon," grew a little weaker.

• • •

A WEEK after we got back from his parents' house, we went out to grab a late lunch in the middle of the afternoon. After lunch, I thought we were headed home, until he took a wrong turn.

"You passed the road," I protested, gesturing out the window after the building flew by.

"Yes, I did. We're not going home," he said, his hand landing on my thigh and squeezing lightly. He'd stopped wearing his suitcoats and ties entirely, sticking with rolling the sleeves of his button-ups the way I'd told him I liked. He'd put less gel in his hair too, emphasizing the waves instead of erasing them, after I mentioned how much I liked them.

"Where are we going, then?"

"It's a surprise."

"You hate surprises, unless they involve sex," I pointed out.

"But you love them, both sexual and nonsexual."

He was right; I did.

I sighed anyway, leaning my head up against the window beside my seat. "Fine, keep your secret."

He chuckled.

A few minutes later, he'd parked in front of a sleek building. I stared out the window at it for a minute, before it registered in my mind exactly why we were there.

"You're buying me a ring?" I asked, my gaze snapping over to him.

"Yes. I need something to sweeten my offer with, and Tatum and Miles agreed that a ring will do the trick."

My eyebrows shot upward. "You can't use my friends against me."

"Technically, I used my sisters-in-law against you."

Touché.

"Come on, Brynlee. It'll be fun." He lifted my hand to his lips and kissed my knuckles lightly.

"I will have very expensive taste in rings," I warned him. "This is not a low-maintenance hand."

He kissed my knuckles again. "Good. The jewelry store rents the building from me, so I'll look like an ass if you pick out something small."

Bash did more work for his real estate venture than he did for the government with the vampire-hunting thing, and made a hell of a lot more money doing it. I hadn't asked him for exact numbers, but it was pretty well known in our friend group that Bash was the richest of the Villins by a long shot. And even the poorest of them was insanely rich, so... yeah.

The bastard probably owned half of Scale Ridge at that point.

"What price should we stay under?" I checked, as he opened my door.

He took my hand, helping me down from the Hummer's passenger seat. "Whatever you want."

I flashed him an annoyed look. "I'm not spending as much on a ring as a damn celebrity would, Sebastian."

"Just pick a ring you love. I don't care about the price." He squeezed my hand, and I bit my lip to hide the smile threatening to break out on my face.

He was too good to me sometimes. Way too good to me.

MY FINGERS DIDN'T FIT in the sample size rings, which made Bash growl at the guys running the shop, but I calmed him down quickly. I hadn't expected that, but it was what it was, even if it was annoying.

We settled for walking around and looking at everything after figuring out my ring size.

As soon as we were back in the Hummer, Bash ordered an excessive number of cheapish rings for me to try on at our house. He wanted me to be able to decide exactly what style I wanted.

On the way home, Bash's hand settled back on my thigh. "I'm taking you to our cabin this weekend."

I lifted my eyebrows at him. "Are you inviting your brothers again?"

I'd been to his cabin once before, during what was basically a couple's trip with me and Bash as awkward fifth and sixth wheels who avoided each other. Zander and Miles had sealed their mate bond, and we'd all celebrated afterward.

"Not a fucking chance."

His answer made me grin.

He squeezed my thigh. "I like to get out of the city every now and then. How do you feel about that?"

I shrugged. "I like vacations. We haven't gone anywhere for your job yet, which surprises me a little."

"I can usually decide whether or not I want to travel. I have enough teams that enjoy it, and they don't need me," he admitted. "It keeps me busy, which is why I usually do it a lot. But I don't need any help staying busy right now." He squeezed my thigh again. "Or in the foreseeable future."

"Haven't you ever heard not to count your chickens before they hatch?" I teased.

"I'll break these chickens out of their eggs myself if they don't hatch."

I snorted, and he couldn't hide his small grin. "Is there an assload of snow up at your cabin right now?"

"Yup. The resort nearby will be busy."

"Miles and Tatum will kill me if we go up there without inviting them on a ski trip, then."

"We're not bringing our family and friends on our first honeymoon, Brynlee. If they've got a problem with our privacy, they can bring it up with me." His voice was firm.

I didn't think he understood the tenacity of my best friends, but decided not to argue with that. Even if I didn't tell them, they'd figure out where we were headed.

"Alright. I'm shitty with skis, though. And worse with snowboards." I shuddered at the memories of landing on my ass repeatedly.

"I'm sure you're better than you think."

"Your certainty is ill-placed, Crash."

"I won't let you fall too many times."

My eyebrows lifted. "We're going to be on our way down a mountain. How are you going to stop me if I start rolling down?"

He considered it.

...And came up with nothing, as expected.

"I'll just stay in the cabin and work." I patted him on the hand. "It'll be nice. I'll have an awesome view."

"The view's fine from our house," Bash pointed out.

"It's different, though."

His forehead pinched slightly. "I'll think of something for us to do off the mountain."

"No way. I saw your snowboard collection in the garage there; you love it. I'll find something for myself to do while you snowboard. Maybe I'll ski with you for a few hours first. I *probably* wouldn't break any bones."

The dirty look he sent me said he didn't like the fact that breaking myself was even a remote possibility.

But it was what it was.

. . .

THE JEWELRY ARRIVED the next day, and Bash sat me down at the table, setting the rings out with cards in front of them to number them.

I raised my eyebrows, taking in the tidy rows. "Wow."

"Welcome to my jewelry shop." He gestured to the rings, sitting down across from me with a notebook.

"Are you going to take notes?"

"Yes." There was no hesitation.

It made me smile.

"You're taking this very seriously."

"If you're going to wear my ring, it's going to be perfect." He picked up ring one.

My smile widened, and I gave him my hand.

A FEW DAYS LATER, we headed up to Bash's cabin.

On the way, I found myself thinking about how strange it was that if I just said I was his when he asked me every night, everything he owned would become mine too.

Dragon shifters made plenty of money, but I hadn't taken anything from my brothers since I moved out to go to college. Before that, they'd taken turns living in Scale Ridge with me while I grew up. The house we'd lived in was modest, and I'd never been allowed to Mate Mountain.

Hell, I didn't even know much about Mate Mountain, the place they all lived. My brothers were careful not to say anything specific to me. I had overheard enough during my childhood to warrant a witch spelling me, so I was unable to talk about what I did know, but it was more annoying than anything given my lack of knowledge.

Most of what I knew was stuff they'd told me about mates.

Mainly, that dragons didn't want them. Dragon shifters were only born male, and if they met their mate, their presence would send the woman into heat. If they could resist easing her heat through sex, they would make it out without sealing the mate bond.

No one ever resisted long enough, though.

I knew my brothers were dragon royalty. It had created contention in the thunder (the name for a pack of dragons) when they refused to let anyone else raise me after our parents died, and others had been trying to overthrow my brothers since. It hadn't happened yet—but I was always nervous it would.

Anyway, the idea of being a part of a demon family that was basically royalty in their own right was a strange one. If the demons had their own leaders, I was confident the Villins would be among them.

Besides that, if I mated with Bash, I would never be alone again. Even if he and I were fighting, my best friends were mated to his brothers. We would be family in every way there was, permanently.

My heart swelled at the idea.

I wanted love, but shit, I ached for that stability.

We were still at our beginning... but maybe our beginning could be a mate bond.

WE REACHED the cabin as the sun was going down, and Bash carried both of our bags inside. We were only planning on staying for a few days, but both of us could work remotely, so there was a chance we'd decide to make the trip a little longer.

"What are you doing?" I checked, following him and our bags into a bedroom on the far side of the massive, gorgeous cabin. It was away from the other three, one of which I assumed I would stay in.

"Putting your stuff in my room. You're sharing my bed while we're here."

I raised my eyebrows at his back. "I am?"

"Yes. You'll be moving into my room when we get home, too."

"Really? I don't remember being asked about that."

He set our bags down at the foot of the bed, then turned to face me. His hands landed on my hips, and he pulled me to his chest. My palms met his pecs, and my fingers pressed lightly against the thick muscles.

Damn, he felt good.

"Brynlee," he said, his voice softening.

"Yes?"

"You're moving into my room." He captured my lips, his hands sliding around to grip my ass.

My fingers dug harder into his pecs, my body warming with his touch and attention.

My chest was rising and falling quickly when I finally made myself pull away. "That still wasn't a request."

He kissed me again, lightly. "No, it wasn't."

My lips curved upward just a little. I couldn't stop the smile. "You're supposed to *ask* me to move in with you, Bash."

He heaved a sigh. "Will you share my room after I've moved your stuff in?"

That was close enough.

"Sure. Sounds like fun."

He kissed me again.

Harder.

When he lifted me off my feet, I wrapped my legs around his ass, pinning his body to mine.

My back hit the wall a moment later, his erection nestled exactly where I wanted it.

"If we're moving in together, you have to feed from me while you're inside me," I said breathlessly.

"Not until you're a demon, baby." His lips and teeth moved down my throat, sucking lightly on my collarbone.

"Sebastian," I groaned, as he gripped one of my breasts.

"I'm not risking you." The words were a growl, his hand releasing my breast and sliding down to the bottom hem of my dress. He tugged it up, out of the way, and pulled my panties to the side. "Ready for me?"

"When am I not?"

He slid a finger inside my channel, stroking my clit with his thumb. "Fucking perfect."

I rolled my hips against his hand. "Give me your cock, Smash."

"It's yours." He freed his erection without bothering to remove his pants, and slid home.

My cries flooded the room, my hips rocking hard as he drove into me. We moved together, the motions growing rougher until we climaxed as one.

The sounds of our pleasure were music to my ears—but as I came down from the high, I wanted more.

I buried my fingers in his hair, dragging his mouth back to mine. He kissed me brutally, his lips and tongue meeting my effort and warring with mine.

He nipped his way down my throat, and I started to move a little again. "Shift for me, Bash."

"No, Brynlee." His growl left no room for question, his lips and teeth toying with my neck.

"If you get to decide I'm moving in with you, I get to decide when you shift. And I want you to shift, now."

"If it didn't put you at risk, I'd do it in a heartbeat."

I groaned in frustration—not pleasure—and my legs tightened around his ass. "It won't put me at risk."

"You don't know that."

"One of my best friends would've mentioned it, don't you think?"

"They have other forms."

"So you think they've never done it in human form?" I demanded.

I felt something hard against my calf, and realized what it was.

His phone.

Leaning against him more, I snagged his phone from his pocket. Typing in the code only took a second, and then I was calling the first person on his recent list.

Rafael answered on the second ring. "Hey."

"Hi Rafe, it's Brynn. Quick question—can you have sex with Tatum while she's in her human form, and you're in your demon form, or does it hurt her?"

There was a beat of silence. "Should I ask why you want to know?"

"Seems pretty obvious," Bash growled into the phone.

"Good point. No, it definitely doesn't hurt her. Do with that what you will. Anything else?"

"Nope. Thanks!" I hung up without waiting for a goodbye, tucking Bash's phone back into the pocket of his slacks. He was still buried inside me, our pleasure dripping down the insides of my thighs.

I flashed him a grin.

"Going to say you told me so?" He dragged a thumb lightly over my chin with the hand that wasn't holding my ass.

"Nah. You know I'm right. That's good enough for me."

His mouth landed on mine again, and I kissed him as he inhaled slowly.

Deeply.

His body grew against mine, and my head tipped back against the wall as my body clenched around his swelling cock.

"Damn," I choked out, every inch of my channel stretched around him.

"That better be a good *damn*."

"So good. Insanely good. Remarkably goo—ohhh." My toes curled as he moved.

My body went still.

He took another deep breath of my lust, and I shuddered.

So close.

I was so close to losing it.

I grabbed his horns, dragging my thumbs over the sensitive tips and making him curse.

"You taste even better wrapped around me like this," Bash growled.

He drove into me.

My hips moved.

And a moment later, we were shattering.

Time became a blur after that.

He feasted on my lust while our bodies moved together.

I had more orgasms than I would've ever guessed was possible.

It was so damn much fun.

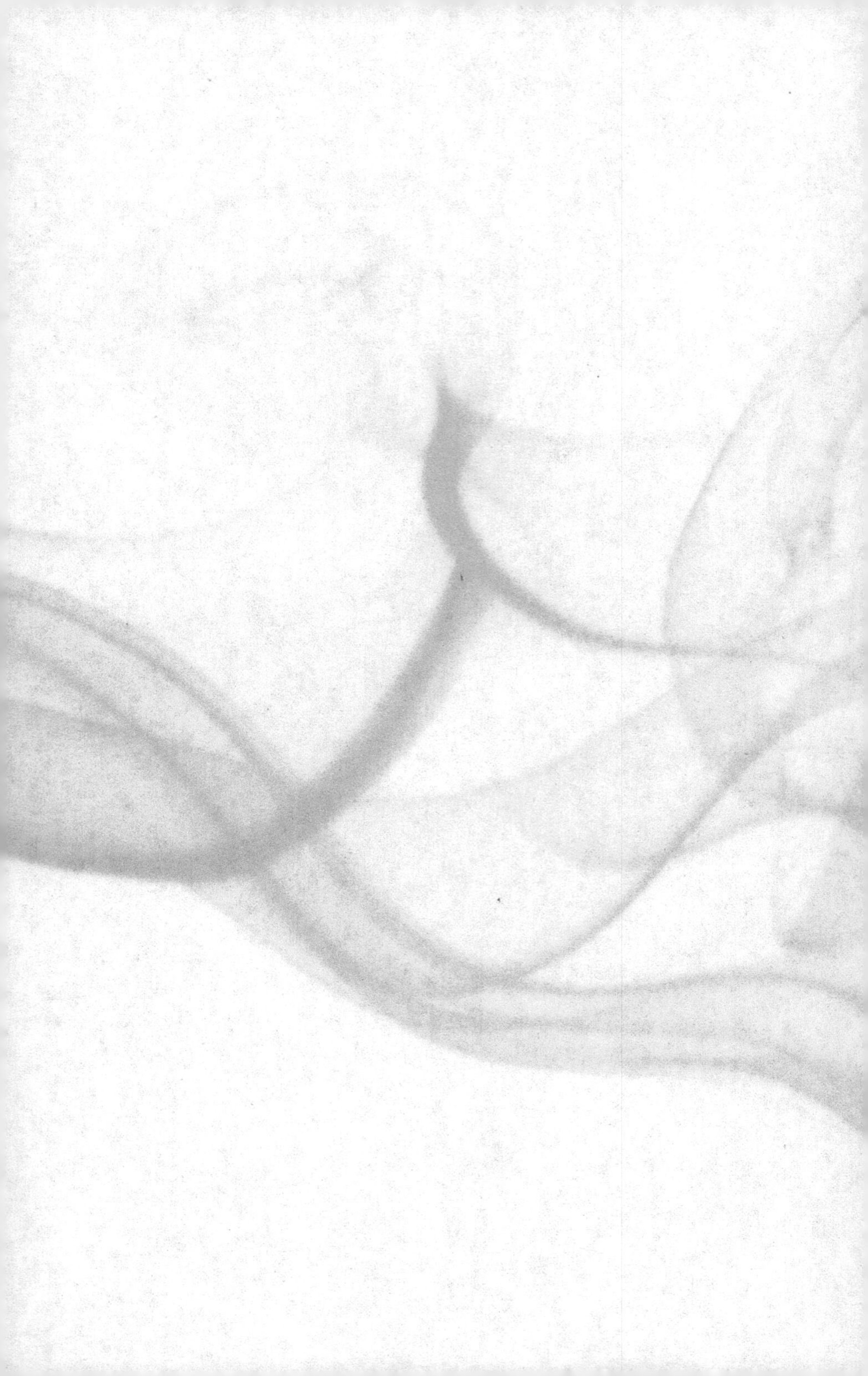

nineteen

BRYNN

WHEN WE FINALLY CALLED IT a night, my stomach was growling ferociously, and my legs were so shaky, I could barely walk. Bash carried me into the shower, and I leaned my face against his chest while he scrubbed both of us clean.

Even after everything we'd done, he still slid his fingers inside me and told me how much he loved my body while he cleaned me.

It made me hot again—and when I had him shift, I buried my fingers in his feathers and made him explode inside me yet again.

Maybe shower orgasms were more fun than I'd realized.

After we were finally dried off, he brushed his lips to my forehead. "Time to feed you."

"I'm fine," I protested, though the words sounded weak. "Let's just go to bed."

My stomach growled again, extra loudly, as if to emphasize my lie.

"Nope." He swept me off my feet, holding me to his chest as he carried me out to the kitchen. I was a little out of it after the sex, and it took me a minute to reorient myself.

We were at his cabin.

Right.

Big windows, more overly-modern furniture.

"I'll never get used to all the square-shaped chairs," I mumbled against Bash's shoulder.

He chuckled. "I know. They're cold and boring, right?"

"I don't think I said it exactly like that..."

"You did.

I grimaced. "Sorry. That was rude."

"Don't apologize. I like that you tell me how you really feel. I'm shitty at guessing games."

"Me too." I leaned my forehead against his neck, closing my eyes at the soft, familiar comfort. "You really don't have to cook for me, though. It's probably the middle of the night."

"It's a little after two AM. I'm just going to boil some pasta. It's not a big deal."

"You're probably going to make sauce from scratch to go over it, though," I grumbled.

His chuckle told me I was right.

"The easiest sauce you know," I warned.

"Alright, baby." He kissed my temple, then set me down on my ass on the countertop.

I leaned my head against the cabinets, lifting my bare feet up to rest on the expensive stone beneath me. I'd put on my typical sleep shirt and a thong, but it wasn't like I felt exposed when the only one with me was Bash.

His hands brushed my skin every time he passed me to grab ingredients or otherwise work on the food. He stroked my knee on his way to fill the pot with water. He squeezed my calf when he reached behind me to grab a spoon. The backs of his fingers grazed my nipple as he stepped past me to pull out a saucepan.

I had never felt loved like that before.

Or important like that.

My eyes stung as I watched him move, touching me every chance he got just because he wanted to.

When his gaze lifted to me, he frowned. "What's wrong?"

"Nothing." I wiped away a few tears.

"Obviously it's not nothing." He dropped his spoon and abandoned both his pasta and the butter he'd started melting.

"It's silly," I said, wiping my eyes.

"I like silly."

I tried to scowl, but mostly failed. "You do not."

He took my face between his hands, his grip gentle. "Tell me."

"It's just..." I bit my lip. "I'm in love with you, Bash. I know it's too soon, but I've never felt like this before. It's over-whelming, but it feels right at the same time. I've never felt this safe, secure, or happy before."

His worry melted away, and a smile stretched his lips. "I'm in love with you too. *Aeternum*, Brynlee." His forehead met mine, and he brushed a kiss to my lips.

Bash didn't expect me to say the word back, or to seal the bond. He would wait as long as I asked him to.

But what was I waiting for? Would I really be any more sure of him tomorrow, or the next week, than I already was?

I didn't think so.

It wasn't like sealing the bond would put an end to our attraction. We would want each other *more* when we were relying on each other for lust.

Or at least, I would want him more. Theoretically. I didn't think it would be possible for him to want me more than he already did.

"*Aeternum*, Bash," I whispered against his lips.

His body stilled.

A wave of pain rolled over me—and heat, with it.

Bash's arms went around my waist, holding me upright as dizziness clouded my mind. My forehead landed on his shoulder, and I held on to him as my body trembled.

"The pasta's going to stick," I mumbled against his skin.

"I don't give a damn about the pasta, baby. You're never getting away from me now. Let me hold you up until you're feeling better; I'm sure the change is intense." His grip on me was firm.

Possessive.

He was mine.

And I really was his. Just one word had been enough to tie us together, permanently.

Well, two words.

"Okay," I said.

He was my mate. If he wanted to hold me while our dinner went to shit, he could hold me. There would be more dinners.

So many more dinners.

And my family—well, my brothers were going to be pissed. But they wouldn't drag me to their prison, and we couldn't be away from each other without causing insanity, so there was nothing they could do about it.

Except possibly hurt Bash.

...We would cross that road when we got there. Hopefully, with my mate's brothers as backup.

The dizziness and shakiness faded after a few minutes, and I finally lifted my head off Bash's shoulder.

"I'm okay," I said. "You can let go."

"I'm not ready yet."

I bit my lip to stop myself from smiling. "The pasta is going to be *really* bad."

"There's a taco shop in town that's open twenty-four hours. It'll only take a few minutes to get there." He turned the stove off and lifted me from the counter, carrying me out to the Hummer. He grabbed a blanket on the way, and wrapped it around me as he held me to his chest.

"I have legs."

"I know. I want them in my hands, along with the rest of you." He squeezed my thigh and ass where he was holding me, but reluctantly set me down when we reached the vehicle.

I'd never imagined a future for myself that involved eating tacos at 2:30 in the morning with my demon soulmate, but honestly, I wouldn't have changed a thing.

THE CABIN'S ringing doorbell had me sitting up quickly, my gaze jerking around the room.

Bash was already tugging pants on and grabbing a weapon out of the closet.

"They rang the doorbell," I hissed, trying to detangle my legs from the blanket. "They wouldn't ring the doorbell if they wanted to hurt us."

His gaze jerked back to me, and moved over my bare figure for a second.

We'd had sex again when we got back. He'd taught me how to feed from him, and it was epic.

Honestly, we were monsters.

"Stay here."

He slammed the door behind him. I heard the front door open while my door was shutting, and rushed out of bed. Bash's button-up was on the ground, so I tugged it over my head before stumbling out after him. The sleeves fell past my hands, but the bottom hem covered everything that needed to be covered, so it was fine.

I stopped in my tracks when I saw Bash a few feet in front of me, and a group of four grinning people in front of *him*.

"We did *not* invite you guys," Bash growled.

"You know better than to go snowboarding without inviting us," Zander drawled. "I own your security system, remember?"

"You created it. I own it." Bash ran a hand through his hair, which was already gorgeously mussed.

"Is that a mate mark?" Tatum asked, her eyes widening as she stared at his hand.

I bit my lip to hide a grin.

I'd watched him touch me with that marked hand in the middle of the night, so yeah, I had already gotten to know it on an *intimate* level.

"It is. We sealed our bond." Bash stepped back beside me, slipping an arm around my waist and smoothing down the fabric of my shirt so I didn't flash anyone.

"Congrats!" Miles exclaimed, and a heartbeat later, she and Tatum were hugging me fiercely tight. "Welcome to the family."

"Have you told your brothers yet?" Tatum asked me. "When did this happen?"

"Last night." They didn't need the details. "And no, I'm just going to let them find out when they get here for Christmas. It'll be more exciting that way." I grinned, and they hugged me tighter.

Immortality with the Villins was going to be a blast.

EVERYONE TALKED me into trying to ski again. After we got dressed and made it to the resort, I reluctantly sat my worried ass on the lift and watched the ground get further and further away.

I was making a pizza with my skis, trying desperately not to fall, when he caught me with a hand on my waist...

Then got down on one knee in front of me.

My eyes watered again, and I waved at the tears, hoping it would stop them from freezing to my eyelids thanks to the insane cold of the mountaintop.

"You're going to marry me, Brynlee," he said, lips curved in a small but wicked smile.

I didn't bother arguing.

And I said yes with my mouth on his, kissing the hell out of him while he slipped the perfect ring on my finger.

WE STAYED at the cabin for a few more days.

I worked more than I spent time on the slopes with everyone, but Bash wasn't letting me out of his sight so soon after sealing the bond. So, we spent the first half of every day with me sucking at skiing, and him snowboarding in circles around me.

Yes, that was an exaggeration, but still.

BASH'S HAND remained on my thigh throughout our drive home, and I couldn't stop myself from looking down at the mate marks on our skin repeatedly.

And smiling.

We were *permanent*. Nothing could change that. And hell, I was a *demon*. It was insane, in the best way.

He made me stay in the Hummer while he opened my door, and as soon as I'd stepped out, he covered my eyes with his hands.

"What are you doing, Crash?"

"Surprising you. For once, don't argue with me."

I laughed, and heard his chuckle too. "I would *never*."

"Of course not. Now, walk with me. Don't try to get ahead; I don't want you tripping over anything."

I obediently walked with him, letting his movements tell me where to go. Mentally, I tried to come up with what the surprise could possibly be.

A house full of roses? Hadn't that been in a romance movie or six? Zander had already done that with Miles, hadn't he?

It seemed excessive, too, but according to Tatum, demons were always excessive.

An engagement-slash-mating cake? If he was buying a cake, he should've brought it to the cabin so everyone else could help us eat it. Then again, Bash could probably kill a cake on his own without much effort, given his sugar addiction.

A... new laptop? Mine worked great, and wasn't old, so that was definitely unnecessary.

Yeah, I was out of ideas.

We walked for a few minutes before Bash finally stopped. "Alright, are you ready?"

"Definitely."

He peeled his hands off my eyes, and I looked out at our living room.

And blinked.

Silence followed.

I could practically feel the worry building in Bash behind me.

"You redecorated for me," I said, my gaze glued to the décor.

It was bohemian, like my coffee shops and my old apartment, but more masculine. There were curtains, the rugs were cozy, and the colors were rich and gorgeous without being gaudy.

More tears stung my eyes.

I really needed to stop crying.

"I did. Well, I paid someone to do it. It's your house too, and I want you comfortable here. I asked Tatum and Miles if I should let you choose everything, but they said you would prefer if it just looked perfect overnight."

A laugh escaped me, and I wiped my eyes. "They're right. This is incredible, Bash." Turning around, I threw my arms around him for a massive hug.

"It's your house too, Brynlee. I want you comfortable and happy here. And you were right; I hated the modern look too." He kissed the top of my head. "We're partners now, for better or worse."

"Let's stick with the better part." I tilted my chin back, and he lowered his lips to mine to kiss me. After a moment, I pulled away and surveyed the room again. "The whole house is redecorated?"

"Yep. All your stuff is already put away in our room, too."

I flashed him a grin. "You're a little wicked, Sebastian."

"Takes one to know one." He kissed me again when I laughed, then draped an arm over my shoulder. "Ready to see the rest of it?"

"So damn ready."

He grinned at me, and I grinned back.

Fuck, I really did love him.

twenty

BRYNN

CHRISTMAS ARRIVED SOON ENOUGH— AND with it, came the dragons.

Bash and I were in the kitchen with his brothers, parents, and my best friends when the doorbell rang.

"Just play it cool," I whispered to Bash, though I was fanning my face.

I, for one, was not playing it cool.

The bastards really might hurt him.

"It'll be fine, Brynlee." Bash grabbed my hand, and I reluctantly let him pull me along. When we reached the door, he tucked me against his side and pulled it open.

All three of my brothers were on the doorstep, wearing their usual grumpy expressions. They all looked nearly identical, with golden skin and blond hair that matched mine. Unlike me, they were covered in tattoos. The tattoos were a shifter tradition of some kind, but they'd never explained it to me.

All three sets of eyes narrowed the moment they saw me and Bash.

Yikes.

"Hey, guys!" I exclaimed, letting go of Bash to throw my arms around all three of them. The bastards were so big, I could barely get my arms around all of them.

My nerves were just going to have to deal with the awkward group hug, because if I wasn't enthusiastic enough, there would be even more fighting.

"Jas, Eli, it's been ages. You should really make it a habit to visit me more often," I said, stepping back beside Bash and slipping an arm around him. His hold on me was loose, but there could be no doubting the possessiveness in it, as always. "August, I've decided to forgive you for playing babysitter for so long. It actually turned out really well."

"What the fuck is on your hand?" August growled at me, taking a menacing step toward me.

Bash didn't flinch.

I didn't either, though I kind of wanted to.

"A mate mark." I lifted my hand cheerfully to show them. "As it turns out, Bash had been fighting the pull of a potential mate bond between us until you moved me into his house. It took some persuading, but I finally convinced him to seal the deal." I winked at August.

August snarled, and stepped toward us again.

"Shit," Jasper muttered under his breath.

Eli set a hand on August's shoulder. "You can't kill the bastard or take him to the prison. They're bonded."

"What do you have to say for yourself, Villin?" August growled.

"You asked me to protect your sister, and there's no better protection than a sealed mate bond. If anyone touches her, they'll die," Bash said bluntly.

I fought the urge to roll my eyes.

Obnoxious, overprotective man.

I couldn't help but love him, though.

"*You* touched her," August bit out.

"Lovingly," I countered.

August all but lunged for us, and Bash tucked me smoothly behind his back.

Then, he shut the door in my face.

I blinked at the wood for all of three seconds before Rafael and Zander got the door open and stepped outside to back Bash up.

The door closed again.

I hesitantly reached for the handle, but my fingers stopped without turning it.

"Brynn, can you make a batch of those peppermint truffles everyone loves while we work on lunch?" Anastasia called, from the kitchen.

My lips curved upward, just slightly. "You don't think I should stop the fight?"

"No, they'll all be in better moods when it's over." Her voice was cheerful; she had definitely recovered from everything that happened over real Thanksgiving. And when I told her my brothers were coming for a do-over of the holiday, she had been eager to have a second chance at it too.

I stepped away from the door, joining them in my kitchen.

As surreal as it had been at first, I loved the way my life had merged with Bash's.

"In better moods, and bleeding, probably," Miles grumbled, as I joined them in the kitchen.

"Soon enough, your brothers will be trying to convince you to have babies too," Anastasia said, winking at me.

I laughed. "In your dreams, maybe."

She grinned, and Eldrich grinned too.

"Be patient," Tatum called, from the pie she was working on. "We're all just enjoying our mates for now."

"Good things come to those who wait, I suppose," Anastasia agreed.

We all worked together, with Christmas music playing from my phone while we chatted and cooked.

Eventually, all six of the guys came shuffling in. As expected, all of them were grinning.

And bleeding, in multiple places.

The soaked part wasn't expected; they were covered in snow, all of it in different stages of melting.

One-by-one, my brothers gave me half-hearted hugs and grumbled their congratulations.

The Villins were grinning even wider when that was over with, and after Bash gave me a quick kiss, everyone disappeared upstairs to grab changes of clothes from my mate.

When they all came down in slacks and button-ups, I couldn't help but laugh.

No way in hell had my brothers ever worn dress clothes.

SOON ENOUGH, we were all eating our makeshift Thanksgiving. After we got everything cleaned up, we exchanged gifts, and played cards for a while before we called it a night.

Anastasia and Eldrich went back to Tatum and Rafael's place with them, and Miles and Zander headed home, leaving me and Bash to say goodbye to my brothers.

"You could've done worse," Eli said, giving me one last hug before clapping Bash on the back. "Take care of her."

"I will."

He strode out, and Jasper pulled me in for a bone-crushing embrace. He'd always given the best hugs.

"Keep an eye on him for us," Jas warned.

I laughed. "Of the two of us, he's not the troublemaker."

He grinned at me as he pulled away, and slapped Bash on the back before he left too.

August studied me for a long moment before he finally gave me a reluctant hug. "You look happy, Brynn," he finally said.

I squeezed him tightly. "I am happy. Trust me to make my own decisions, now."

He let out a long sigh. "Alright."

He released me, shook Bash's hand, and finally left us alone.

Our door shut behind him, and I stepped up to Bash's side, leaning against him. His arms went around me, and he pulled me in close, kissing the top of my head. "That went well."

"It did. How bad are your cuts?"

"Not bad at all. Their hearts weren't in it. You were too damn happy for them to really hate me." He pulled me closer. "I have your present in the garage."

"I told you not to get me anything," I protested.

"I ignored that request." He kissed my head again.

"Well, I ignored it too. Your presents are in our closet."

He laughed, towing me out to the garage.

My eyes widened when I saw his usual black Hummer—parked right beside an identical but bright yellow one, with a big red bow on the top.

"I figured it was time to replace your car," he said, his voice light. "Miles and Tatum told me you've always wanted a yellow one, but have never been willing to fork over the money for something brand new so you can pick the color."

Tears stung my eyes, and I threw my arms around Bash, squeezing him hard. "She's perfect, Smash. Thank you so much."

"Of course." He tilted my head back, and kissed me. "The other half of your gift is your first flying lesson. I wasn't sure how to wrap that one up, either."

"You're the best." I kissed him again, harder. "I love you. My presents are going to seem crappy, now."

"They won't." He squeezed my hand.

Though I sighed, I towed him up the stairs and into our closet. When I ordered him to sit on the bed while I retrieved said presents, he sat.

I came out with two wrapped gifts, and handed them both over to him. He made quick work of opening them, and I bit my lip while he held up some of the fabric. A smile curved his lips when he realized what the clothes were, and his eyes met mine. "Sweats and t-shirts?"

I met his smile with my own. "You really haven't experienced true comfort without them. Now, you can actually be comfortable when we sit on the couch together. I even sent them to your tailor, so you should be happy with the way they fit, too."

He chuckled, the sound rich and happy, as he set the gifts down and pulled me back into his arms. He kissed me slowly, his body pressed to mine as our tongues tangled. "Thank you, Brynlee," he murmured against my lips. "I love you."

"I love you too." I rested my forehead against his neck.

Life was good.

So, so good.

And knowing it was never going to end only made me feel even better.

"HERE, take Elle. Annie wants more potatoes," Brynn said, putting our one-year-old in my arms. Elle gave a battle-shriek, and smacked me in the face with the plastic doll she'd taken from one of her older sisters. With four daughters, there were a plethora of girly, pink toys everywhere, and I loved every minute of it.

I'd never realized how damn much I'd love being a dad, but those little girls had me wrapped around their tiny, adorable fingers.

I grinned at Elle, not bothering to take the doll. "You're a warrior."

"She is. And she's mine," Tatum declared, sweeping the little girl away from me.

Tatum was eight-months pregnant with her second. Brynn, Tatum, and Miles had all gotten pregnant around the same time seven years earlier. While Tatum and Miles both had boys, Brynn had a girl.

And another girl, a year-and-a-half after the first.

And a third, two years after that.

And a fourth, a year-and-a-half later.

Our daughters were just like their mother; wild, sweet, and fun.

Miles and Zander had three boys. The oldest two were six and three, and their youngest was a newborn. Our mother had him cradled in her arms while she and our dad chatted with the couple on the couch. Their other kids were running around with ours in the toy room. They were all close, and could entertain each other for days without intervention, as long as there were snacks nearby.

Tatum and Rafael were expecting a girl, and I had no doubt she would be partners in crime with our little Elle.

My gaze followed Brynn to the kitchen, and my lips curved as I watched her chat with our two-year-old as she put together another plate of food.

My girls loved their mother so much, it made my chest ache. It was so damn good to see them together.

"Who would've thought my trip to prison would lead to all of this?" Rafael asked, stepping up beside me and draping an arm over my shoulder. His eyes followed his mate, flicking toward the toy room when a few kids ran out with pink foam swords in their hands.

"Not me. I was so damn pissed when you took the fall for us."

He grinned. "Glad about it now, though, huh?"

"Undoubtedly." I watched Brynn help Annie to the table, and sit down with her. Rafael's year in hell had led to a lifetime of everything I hadn't realized I wanted or needed. "Ready for the new baby?"

Rafe grinned, his smile nearly blinding. "Hell yes."

I chuckled. "Good."

Brynn tucked a few strands of hair behind Annie's ear, and my chest ached again.

She was so damn perfect for me.

"I'm going to go help my mate. Bring my kid back when Tatum's done with her."

"Will do." Rafael smacked me on the back as I ducked out from beneath his arm, striding across the room.

Annie squealed and lunged for me when I sat down on the bench next to Brynn, and I caught her easily.

"Hey, baby." I kissed Brynn lightly, while Annie climbed all over me like I was a wall she needed to scale.

Brynn smiled. "Hey, Smash." She snagged Annie from me, earning a banshee-like scream that made us both grin.

I fucking loved our life.

afterthoughts

Awww.

Sigh.

This one gave me all the feels. I'm not sure if people still say that, but whatever. I'm saying it.

Brynn and Bash were a little more... volatile... than the other couples in this series, but I had SO much fun with their story, and I hope you loved it too.

Thank you so much for joining me on this journey with the Villins and our coffee-shop-running candy makers! Their stories made me smile and snort to myself way too many times, and I loved every minute of it!

I'm nowhere near done with this world. Maybe sexy PNR romcoms are my new calling in life...

Hmm.

Only time will tell!

I have a series planned for Brynn's brothers, but first, I'll be taking a detour to Wildwood. I hope you go with me! Book 1 in that series is called The Art of Avoiding a Werewolf.

Thank you so much for reading!
All the love,
Lola Glass <3

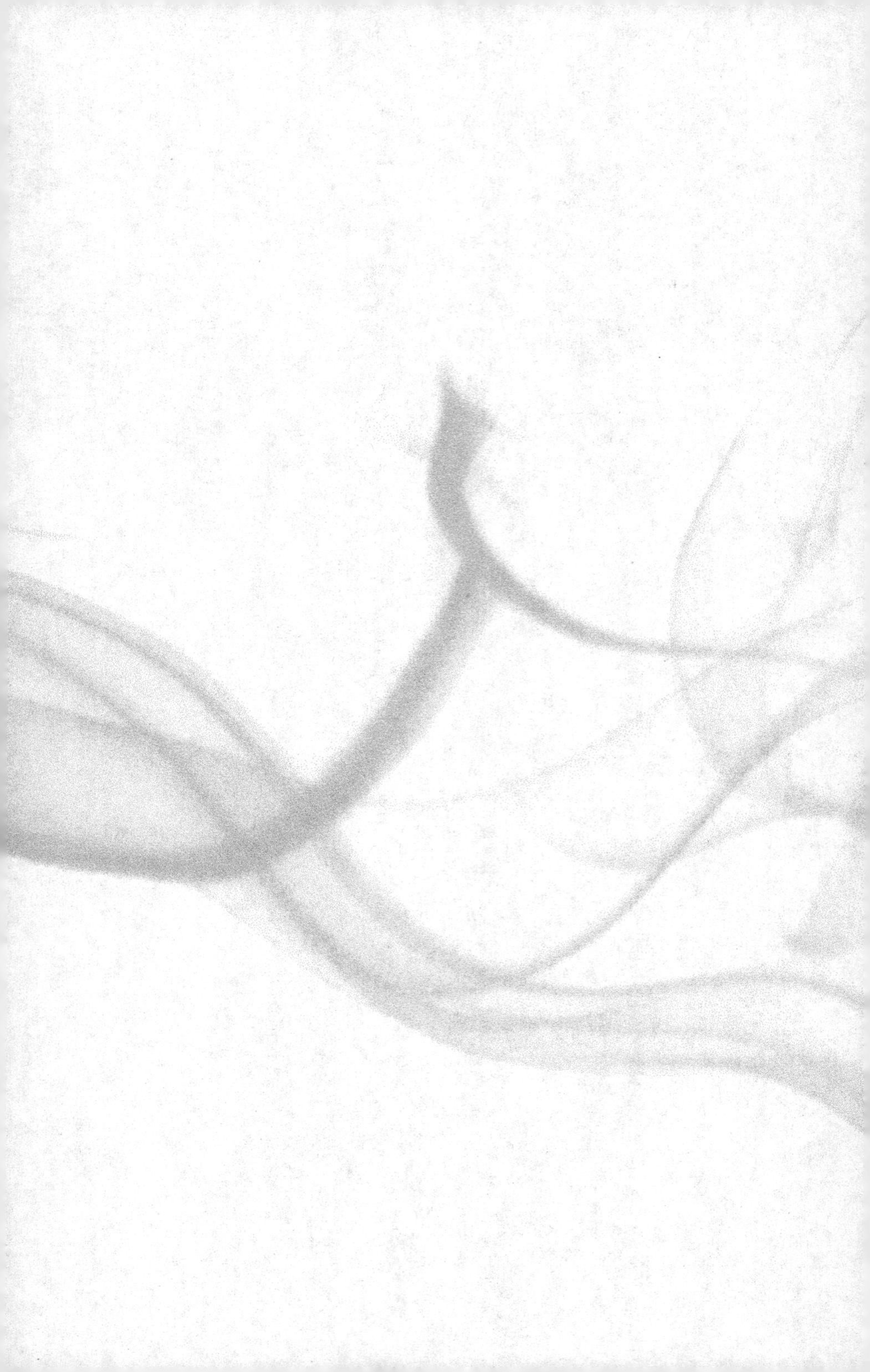

stay in touch

If you want to receive Lola's newsletter for new releases (no spam!) use this link:

LINK

Or find her on:
FACEBOOK
TIKTOK
INSTAGRAM
PINTEREST
GOODREADS

about the author

Lola is a book-lover with a *slight* romance obsession and a passion for love—real love. Not the flowers-and-chocolates kind of love, but the kind where two people build a relationship strong enough to last. That's the kind of relationship she loves to read about, and the kind she tries to portray in her books.

Even though they're fun stories about sassy women and huge, growly magical men ;)